Copyright © 2022 E S Monk

Published 2022

ISBN 9798784138019

Hollybrook Stables

Inherited Horse

By

E.S. Monk

For

Jess and Jenny

Clare

Clare was holding back her tears as she tightly gripped the steering wheel of her battered old green Land Rover. *They are happy tears,* she kept telling herself. *This is such a wonderful opportunity for them. I'm thrilled for them, really, I am. And six months isn't forever, the time will fly by.* She was determined not to dwell on the fact that her house would seem woefully quiet now that she had just dropped off her beloved son Joe, his wonderful girlfriend Riley, and Riley's little sister Molly, off at Heathrow airport, and they were about to board a plane bound for Australia.

"It was me who encouraged them to go!" she said out loud. She herself had found the advert in one of her horsey magazines.

Young couple wanted:

Yard work, maintenance work, horse training and riding needed

on busy show jumping yard. Accommodation provided. Sydney, Australia.

"What an adventure you would have!" she had encouraged them, waving the advert in their faces as soon as she saw it. It didn't take Joe and Riley long to realise what a fantastic opportunity it would be, and they applied for the position the next day.

Two weeks later, and here she was, bawling her eyes out as she tootled along the motorway, heading home to Hollybrook stables.

She thought back to how her life could have been so different, how she would have loved to have travelled the world whilst she was young. But things hadn't turned out that way. *I wouldn't change a thing,* she thought, smiling to herself.

Clare's parents had passed away when she was twenty. They struggled for years to have a baby of their own, and finally, when they had all but given up hope, her mum fell pregnant with her at the age of forty-five. Her father was fifty-four when she was born. Clare smiled as she thought back to the wonderful childhood her parents had given her. Although elderly, they doted on her in every way. She was born and raised at Hollybrook, and her life was filled with love, horses and lots of home-made cake.

Clare's idyllic world fell apart when her father suffered a fatal stroke at the age of seventy-four. Her mother, forever devoted to her father, never fully recovered from his loss and five months later, she died of what Clare could only assume was a broken heart.

Consumed with grief and overwhelmed with the responsibility of taking over Hollybrook stables on her own, Clare went decidedly off the rails for the next six months. Her days were filled with riding, and her nights with drinking and partying. She did whatever she could to block out the pain and misery she was enveloped in after her tragic loss. Then along came Peter. How foolish she had been. Seeking comfort and feeling reckless, she did what she never thought she would do; she had a one-night stand. She regretted it instantly and sneaked out of his flat as soon as he fell into a deep, drunken slumber next to her. *This is not the way my parents brought me up,* Clare thought, chastising herself as she walked home in the early hours of the morning in her torn mini dress. *They would be horrified at my behaviour. Enough. It's time to start taking my responsibilities seriously,* she told herself firmly. And she did. From that day on, she bucked up her ideas, kept the house and yard clean, and started to take on horses for training. Then one morning, whilst grooming horses on the yard, she felt nausea flooding through her, and she promptly threw up into an empty feed bucket.

It took a whole week for her to pluck up the courage and tell Suzie. Remembering it now, Clare felt grateful for their many years of friendship; Suzie truly was the most wonderful, loyal friend that anyone could wish for. Suzie had immediately told her to take a pregnancy test, then waited with her as they sat and sipped their mugs of tea at her kitchen table for the agonizing three minutes, staring blankly at the pregnancy test. Slowly but surely, the second pink line started to show.

After the initial shock, and three cups of tea later, Clare accepted the news and made the decision to be happy about it. After such devastating loss, her very own baby started to feel like a blessing. Of course, she contacted Peter and explained the situation. He, however, was now back at university and a baby was most definitely not in his plans. He very firmly told her, in no uncertain terms, that if she wanted it, she took responsibility for it. It was nothing to do with him. Clare never saw or heard from Peter again, and she was fine with that state of affairs. When Joe arrived, her beautiful baby boy, she knew that she didn't want to share him with anyone anyway. As soon as she held him in her arms, she promised Joe, and herself, that she was going to give him the type of childhood her parents gave her, filled with love, horses and lots of home-made cake. And to the best of her knowledge, she had.

Clare sniffed and wiped a lone tear from her face with the back of her hand, as she turned the car into the driveway. It was nice to be home – this place held so many happy memories. Suddenly feeling positive again, she climbed out of her car and headed onto the yard. There was work to be done, after all.

Suzie

Suzie and her sons, John and Joseph, were seated in the audience at the Hickstead Royal International Horse Show. The atmosphere was electric, and all the spectators were buzzing with excitement as they watched the fearless show jumpers take on the enormous jumps in the ring.

Suzie made the four-and-a-half-hour trip from Cornwall especially, because Luke, her boyfriend, would be competing with his horse Gilly. He had given her three tickets so she and the boys could enjoy a great day out, watch him compete and then as a final treat, he was going to take them all out for pizza after the show. The boys were beyond excited.

Suzie glanced over at her boys. They were spellbound watching the spectacular show of skill, proficiency and talent the professional show jumpers were displaying. Then they heard Luke's name announced over the show speaker.

"He's next!" said John animatedly, as Joseph wriggled in his seat with excitement.

Then they saw them. *What a smart pair they look*, Suzie thought smugly. They were the most handsome horse and rider, by far. Gilly was positively gleaming, oozing presence and power as he trotted around the ring. Luke, focused and in control, looked gorgeous in his impeccably white breeches and smart navy-blue jacket, Suzie could see the gold buttons shining from where she was sitting, far away in the crowd. His black leather boots were buffed and polished to perfection. He and Gilly were a formidable team. They all heard the bell ring, and then they were off, cantering effortlessly around the ring. Suzie held her breath as Luke and Gilly headed towards the first double spread. He had him going in a nice steady canter. She released her breath as they elegantly soared over the first jump. They approached the second, bigger than the first with two bright purple fillers. Once again, the dynamic pair sailed over the jump in perfect style. Suzie began to relax. Luke and Gilly clearly knew what they were doing. *This is what they do,* she told herself. *Stop worrying, sit back and enjoy the show.* Suzie, the boys and the crowd cheered Luke on as he successfully cleared the third jump.

And then it happened. Suzie felt like the world had gone into slow motion and the once- jubilant crowd silenced as the sound of the jumps clattering to the ground echoed in the air, followed by a sickening crunch as Luke and Gilly crumbled to the earth in a tangled heap.

Gilly struggled to his feet, shook himself off and surveyed the scene around him. The crowd looked on in horror as he put his nose down to Luke and sniffed him. Luke didn't move a muscle. He was lying splayed out on the floor, motionless. The paramedic crew leapt into action and raced onto the scene. A low hubbub rippled through the crowd. Suzie waited, along with the whole arena, to see if Luke would get up. He didn't. The paramedics carefully rolled him on to a stretcher and carried him out of the ring.

Suzie felt a wave of nausea sweep over her, as she gathered up the boys. They fought their way through the crowds, being jostled from all sides, as they struggled to reach Gilly's designated stable. She felt a deep sense of terror, in the very pit of her stomach, as she desperately tried to find someone who could tell them what was going on.

Eventually an official approached, as they anxiously waited outside Gilly's stable.

"Luke is unconscious," he said gravely. "He's been taken to hospital."

Ellen

Ellen was schooling Sundance, Riley's horse. After having her application accepted for the six-month job opportunity in Australia, Riley asked Ellen if she would take on Sundance and treat him as her own until her return. Ellen jumped at the chance. Sundance was Riley's pride and joy, and Ellen felt extremely flattered to have been offered the responsibility of caring for him whilst she was away. She could hardly believe her luck. He was a fantastic school master and jumper, and she knew that the next six months of training him and taking him to shows was going to be great fun!

A small country show was being held at the weekend, so Ellen and Sundance were practicing for the four-foot jumping class.

If we nail this show, then we'll be entering the five foot in a couple of weeks! Ellen thought happily as she transitioned from trot to canter and pointed Sundance at the five-foot straight bar ahead of them. Confidently and carefully, they cleared it with ease.

"That's it, boy," Ellen murmured to Sundance as she gently patted his neck.

Ellen and Sundance were lost in their own world, training hard in the sand school, when all of a sudden, a massive commotion came from the feed room, causing Sundance to spook. He swiftly spun round to face what had caused such a ruckus. The banging and crashing continued, Sundance's concentration on the schooling session now long gone, and after his previous clear jump, Ellen decided to call it a day. She dismounted, led Sundance out of the school and tied him up on the yard. She needed to investigate what was causing such a commotion, although she already had a fairly good idea as to what it might be.

Peeking around the feed room doorway she saw the culprit, Molly's pony. Fat little Pipsqueak was at it again.

"How on earth did you escape from your paddock this time, you little monster?" Ellen affectionately said to the hairy, skewbald Shetland pony, who was munching his way through what was supposed to be their winter hay supply. Pipsqueak looked up at her with innocent, liquid brown eyes, completely in denial that he was part of any wrongdoing.

"How can I be cross with that little face?" said Ellen as she picked up his bright pink sparkly head collar, with the plan of catching him and taking him back to his field. Pipsqueak had other ideas, though. As soon as he saw the headcollar, he was off. He scooted out of the feed room quick as lightning, and Ellen was secretly impressed that such a fat little pony could move so fast. Pipsqueak went crashing through the yard and was dancing in circles around the carpark when she finally caught up with him, his naughty little eyes glinting with mischief at her.

"Pipsqueak, you get back here right now!" hollered Ellen.

Clare

Clare had been watching the drama with Pipsqueak unfold from her kitchen window. After laughing uncontrollably to herself, she regained her composure and went outside to help Ellen try to capture the wild, hairy beast that went by the name of Pipsqueak.

"The little terror needs a job to do," laughed Ellen. "Ever since Molly left, he's been even more naughty than usual. We'll have six months of this if you don't find a way to keep his mind busy."

"I one hundred percent agree with you," chuckled Clare in reply.

Creasing up with laughter at the chaos Pipsqueak was causing, eventually, they managed to wrestle the headcollar on to him and escort him back to his paddock.

Exhausted after chasing and then capturing the little runaway, Clare and Ellen settled down for a rest and much needed cup of tea in Clare's kitchen and started plotting ideas to try and curb Pipsqueak's wayward behaviour.

"What if I lead him when I hack out with Sundance? Sundance won't put up with any of his antics. He can keep him in line for us."

"Great idea! Some nice long hacks ought to tire the little rascal out."

Through the kitchen window, Clare and Ellen saw a horse box heading up the drive, followed by a silver Volvo.

"That's my new livery," exclaimed Clare, jumping to her feet. She was glad that the latest drama with Pipsqueak had been resolved before they arrived. She at least liked to put on the pretence of running a professional yard and preferred any new clients to be well and truly settled in before witnessing the chaos caused by the resident yard jester!

David

David felt like he was on auto pilot. The death of his mother five days ago had hit him hard. He'd known it was coming, so he thought he would be prepared when his mother closed her eyes for the last time and the doctor nodded his head at him, a silent gesture explaining she had gone. She had been unwell for a long time but had deteriorated quickly over the last two months. They both agreed, though, that at least this way, they were given the chance to say all the things they wanted to say to each other, and to spend the last weeks of her life together, content within each other's company. Something that was robbed from many others, whose lives can end so cruelly and abruptly. David took comfort from the fact he and his mother did not waste the last days of her life together. They enjoyed what time they had left as best they could, even though they knew that the end was coming soon

It had always just been him and his mother. He had once asked questions about his father. His mother had told him, in a very matter of fact manner, that while she had been desperately in love with his father, he was a married man, and that was the part that she regretted. The relationship had been nothing more than an illicit affair, and they had both felt an immediate sense of unbearable guilt once the affair started. It had ended swiftly, neither of them realising that her pregnancy was the result. However, his father never regaled on his parental duties financially, generously supporting them both until David turned eighteen. But the decision had been made that it was best for everyone if his only contributions were financial. David was to be brought up by his mother, and his mother alone. At the time, and still to this day, David appreciated his mother's complete honesty when asked about his father. He respected her for it, and not once did he feel the need to seek out his father or find out more about who he was. He had always been happy with just his mother, and the truth about where he came from enabled him to feel content with his lot in life.

The legalities of his mother's will were all in order. David was a solicitor, so that part had been easy, and he had taken it all in his stride. It helped, having something practical to focus on during those first, hauntingly empty days after her death. The second matter, however, made David feel completely out of his depth. Aside from himself, his mother's other great love in life was horses. Irish drafts were her preferred breed and throughout his life, his mother was never without a horse.

Daisy Mae was by far her favourite. She was a gentle, placid, 16.3 stamp of a mare, and the love of his mother's life. His childhood memories were filled with happy times, playing on the yard where Daisy Mae lived, his mother leading him bareback around the fields until they found the perfect picnic spot. Daisy Mae would graze whilst he and his mother tucked into delicious home-made sandwiches and cake. He smiled fondly at the memories whenever they came to him.

Daisy Mae was sent away for a month, and on her return, she was treated like even more of a queen than usual. Three months later, after a much-anticipated visit from the vet, his mother's wish came true. Her darling mare was in foal. By this time, David was away at university. He remembered laughing at his mother on the phone and telling her she was suffering from empty nest syndrome. In his mother's typical, honest, matter of fact way, giggling her reply, she admitted that she most definitely was, and Daisy Mae was going to help her fill the void.

After a further agonizing seven month wait, Captain was born, the apple of both his mother's and Daisy Mae's eyes. The years passed and David finished university, worked in a selection of different firms to gain experience, then at the age of thirty-two, set up his own firm in a bustling little town, not far from his mother's home, near the Cornish moors. It was a sad day for everyone when Daisy Mae closed her eyes, in her comfortable, warm stable, for the last time. She'd lived a long and happy life, but her time had finally come.

His mother often said, during the last few weeks of her life, that she wasn't afraid. She was going to be with Daisy Mae again, and that thought brought her comfort during the long painful nights her illness engulfed her in.

David's predicament now, though, was what to do with Captain? Although he was brought up with horses, he didn't actually know that much about them. He enjoyed their company, but horses were really his mother's passion, and without her, he felt completely overwhelmed. Captain was now in his prime, a handsome, twelve-year-old, 16 hand, pure bred Irish draft, dapple grey gelding, David didn't know if he could do justice to this magnificent horse. A friend of a friend had suggested that he move Captain to a livery yard, where they could take care of his daily needs, which would then give David time to decide what to do in the long run for Captain's best interest.

And that was how he found himself now, following a horsebox, driving across the countryside to a place called Hollybrook stables.

Jem

Jem's breath caught in her throat as she listened to Suzie trying to explain the devastating news about Luke over the phone. She was struggling to speak coherently. She was at the hospital now, and the doctors were with Luke. She was waiting for news about his condition. The boys, understandably, were in shock, as they had seen the terrible accident take place. Jem could tell that Suzie didn't know what to do next; she was going out of her mind with worry.

Jem took charge of the situation for her. She took control of her own fear and put on her most calm, confident voice.

"I'm on my way," she told Suzie. "I'll swing by the yard, check Pandora, and of course I'll check Clarissa for you, then I'll explain to Clare what's going on. I'll bring the horse box as well. Dealing with Gilly will be one less thing that you have to worry about."

Jem heard a sigh of relief down the phone.

"Thank you, Jem," Suzie said hoarsely. "I knew you'd be the best person to make sense of it all and come up with a practical plan."

On arriving at the yard, Jem saw a beautiful, dapple grey Irish draft being led out of a horse box.

Oh no, what awful timing, thought Jem as she remembered that Clare was expecting a new livery today. *I'll sort Pandora and Clarissa out first,* she decided. *Then I'll break the news to Clare about what's happened.*

Jem efficiently went about her horse care duties and within twenty minutes, Pandora and Clarissa were happily munching grass out in their paddock. *I can't put it off any longer,* she thought, as she walked over to Clare, Ellen and the man who must be the new livery.

Calling Clare away from the others, she quickly relayed the most important bits of Suzie's catastrophic news. Clare immediately swung into action. The Land Rover was backed up and securely hitched to the horse trailer, a flask of tea and cake tin were placed on the passenger seat and Jem was instructed to get in. Clare was most definitely coming with her to the hospital. She gave David a quick explanation of what was happening, then jumped into the car.

The poor man, Jem thought, as Clare, next to her, put the Land Rover into gear.

"He does look a bit bewildered, doesn't he," Clare said, preparing to drive off.

"I'm leaving you in very capable hands," Clare called out of the window. "Ellen is here, she's the yard's riding instructor. She'll sort everything out and make sure Captain is ok until I get back."

Then, with a brief wave, Clare and Jem sped out of the driveway.

Suzie

Suzie's mind was spinning as she struggled to comprehend what the doctor was trying to tell her. It was hard to focus, amongst the constant beeping of the machines Luke was hooked up to and the busy nurses, working hard as they bustled around her.

"Induced coma... traumatic brain injuries...bruised ribs.... we just have to wait and see." All she could hear from the doctors was a string of words, and her muddled mind was struggling to grasp the severity of the situation.

Suzie stared blankly at Luke, as he lay there with wires and tubes sticking out of him. It was too much to take in, too much to bear. *How could such a wonderful day lead to such a devastating end?* Unstoppable tears rolled down her pale cheeks.

She sat next to Luke's hospital bed, holding his hand. After a while, she was approached by a kindly-looking nurse, offering her a cup of tea, who introduced herself as Emma.

"I'm taking over Luke's care for the next shift," Emma said gently. "Down here, in the intensive care unit, Luke will receive twenty-four-hour care. He will have a nurse with him at all times, and for the next twelve hours, that will be me. I'm happy to answer any questions you might have, and I'll do my best to support you whilst we wait to find about more about Luke's condition." Emma gave Suzie's arm a gentle, supportive squeeze, then got on with her job of caring for Luke.

Suzie wasn't sure how much time had passed, when another nurse came and called her out of the intensive care unit, informing her that she had some visitors. On seeing Clare and Jem waiting for her outside, she collapsed into Jem's outstretched arms and cried and cried, as if her heart would break.

"Where are the boys?" Clare asked.

Suzie smiled weakly. She knew that Clare struggled in overly emotional situations, always preferring to be practical and kept busy until the crux of the situation presented itself. And, at the moment, the doctors didn't know anything, so Clare would simply be practical until told otherwise.

"With one of the nurses," Suzie replied. "They didn't think it a good idea for them to see Luke in the intensive care unit, so they've been taken for a sandwich at the hospital café."

"I'll go and find them," Clare announced, and after giving Suzie a brief hug, she was gone.

"I've spoken to the doctors," Jem said. "They said that you were still in shock and might not have digested all of the information they gave you. Would you like me to be there next time you speak to them? Would it help to have me by your side whilst they explain to you again what's happening?"

Suzie, through broken sobs, replied, "thank you, Jem. I understand that Luke hit his head when he fell. If it hadn't been for his riding hat, the damage would have been much more severe, possibly fatal. He has suffered a traumatic brain injury. His brain has swollen inside his skull, so they have put him in an induced coma to try and prevent any more swelling. Once the swelling subsides, then they'll bring him out of the coma, and only then will they know if there is any brain damage, and what the extent of that might be."

Suzie felt Jem's arms circle around her again, and relaxing into her embrace she felt a small blanket of comfort shroud her as Jem quietly soothed her. From then on, all they could do was wait.

Ellen

Ellen didn't quite know what to make of David. He was perfectly pleasant and polite but he seemed somewhat distant and distracted in his current surroundings. Captain, everything in his wardrobe, and all his feed buckets were immaculate. He was clearly very well looked after and had a good temperament. He was gentle and calm, even after his journey and move to a new yard. Ellen thought he was a very beautiful horse indeed.

Ellen was explaining to David the routine she thought would be best for Captain, when his phone rang. He offered a quick apology and explained that it was work, then stepped away to answer the call, giving Ellen the opportunity to study him properly without his knowledge. He was about six feet tall, and slim, with neatly cropped brown hair and gold-rimmed spectacles. *He looks like the studious sort*, she thought, watching him closely.

"I'm going to have to go I'm afraid," said David, putting his phone back in his pocket. "I've just been called into an urgent meeting."

Ellen looked at him, unimpressed that he could possibly drop his horse off at a new yard and not stay long enough to settle him in. Out loud, she said, "No problem, I'll sort everything out." It wouldn't do to be rude to one of Clare's clients. *If I have nothing nice to say, I won't say anything at all,* she thought, and with a curt nod, she strode off towards the feed room to organise Captain's things.

She heard his Volvo start up and drive away from the yard.

She turned to Captain. "Well, aren't you a handsome boy," she said, and gently tickled his nose.

Ellen didn't even bother to turn around, when she heard the banging and crashing that shortly followed.

"Hello, Pipsqueak," she said simply.

Clearly the nosey little munchkin wanted to investigate who the new creature standing on his yard was, and Ellen didn't have the heart to shoo him away. Instead, she turned back to Captain.

"You might as well get to know the little monster now," she giggled affectionately. "He'll terrorize you one way or another, so best to be prepared for the onslaught."

To her surprise, when little Pipsqueak marched right up to Captain and shoved him with his nose, Captain, didn't even acknowledge him. Pipsqueak tried his rude introduction a second time, and again, nothing from the big horse.

"Why don't you try being nice," Ellen suggested to him.

Another nudge, still no response from Captain. Pipsqueak, unused to being ignored, stood quietly next to Captain whilst he planned his next move, but Captain outwitted him. As soon as he was calm and quiet, he faced Pipsqueak and gently snuffled him.

"Well, well, well," said Ellen. "Looks like you've met your match now, little man."

She untied Captain's lead rope and led him out to the paddock, with Pipsqueak hot on their heels. "Do you want to go in here with Captain?" Ellen asked the little pony, as she held the gate open for him to follow. Nonchalantly walking through the gate of his own accord, Pipsqueak glued himself to Captain's side. Ellen closed the gate and watched as Captain and Pipsqueak settled together in the paddock. If Captain moved, Pipsqueak moved. If Captain grazed, Pipsqueak grazed. Pipsqueak always positioned himself at no more than three feet away from Captain. *How funny,* mused Ellen. *The little mischief maker has found himself a friend.* Smiling to herself at this new turn of events, she left the horses and headed back to the yard.

Clare

Clare was sitting on a bale of hay outside the stable Gilly was currently residing in, waiting for Rose, the vet, to arrive. Gilly had been given the all-clear by the show vet on the day of the accident, but Clare just wanted him double checked, and if Rose agreed that he was alright, then she would finally be able to relax.

When she saw Rose's car trundling up the drive, she clipped the lead rope to Gilly's headcollar and led him onto the yard for Rose to examine him.

"Hi Clare," Rose called out as she closed her car door and walked over towards her and Gilly. "I couldn't believe it when I heard about Luke and Gilly. It's the sort of accident we all know is possible, but never believe will actually happen. How is Luke?"

"It's an absolute tragedy, Rose," Clare replied gravely. "He's still in intensive care. I spoke to Suzie earlier today. The doctors are pleased with his progress, even though it's slow going. They're hoping to bring him out of the coma any day now."

Rose got straight to the business at hand and started to examine Gilly. She ran her hands all over his body and down his legs, listened to his heart with her stethoscope and then watched carefully as Clare trotted him up and down the yard.

"He seems to be in perfect health to me. I definitely agree with the show vet's initial assessment," announced Rose.

"Well, that's a relief!" sighed Clare, "I'll turn him out so he can have a good stretch of his legs then."

Rose followed Clare as she led Gilly away from the yard and towards his paddock. "Isn't it strange," Rose said. "Both Gilly and Luke were involved in the same terrible accident, yet there isn't a mark on Gilly and Luke is in hospital fighting for his life."

"Life can be so very unfair," replied Clare, as she unclipped and slipped off Gilly's headcollar, then watched as he took off hell for leather, bucking and squealing across his paddock.

"At least he's healthy and happy," Rose said, smiling at Gilly's exuberant antics.

"Indeed, and Suzie will be able to tell Luke how fit and healthy Gilly is as soon as he wakes up," replied Clare, praying as she said the words that that day would come very soon.

David

David's friends told him to be ready by ten o'clock on Saturday morning. They were going out for the day, and they weren't taking no for an answer. He knew they were trying to be nice by keeping him busy to take his mind off the loss of his mother, but he was rather keen to visit Captain at Hollybrook, and hopefully, bump into Ellen. He felt that when he left her the other day, she seemed to somehow disapprove of him, and he didn't like it. He thought if they would be bumping into each other on the yard, he didn't want there to be any awkwardness. Plus, since he knew so little about horses, any advice the ladies at Hollybrook could offer him would be received most gratefully, so falling out with one of them was not in his best interest at all.

He diplomatically decided to get up early on his day off and arrived at Hollybrook for eight thirty. The yard was a hive of activity, just as he thought it would be, but disappointingly, there was no sign of Ellen. He introduced himself to a very friendly lady called Jem, and watched in admiration as she somehow managed, in a very short time indeed, to groom and tack up two large ponies, with three very excited boys playing around her. She politely pointed him in the direction of Captain's paddock, before allowing the boys to climb onto the ponies, then the little party strode off down the drive for a ride. *Blimey, two horses and three children,* David thought. *I don't even know where to start with one horse.*

David found Captain with a very hairy little pony at his side. He enjoyed stroking Captain's silky soft mane and meeting his miniature friend in the paddock, but with his equine skills desperately found wanting, he made no attempt to take him out of the paddock and on to the yard. He stayed for as long as he could, but still there was no sign of Ellen. Feeling somewhat dejected, he said his goodbyes to Captain and left the yard in order to be on time to meet his friends.

At twelve thirty, David was sitting outside the beer tent at the local agricultural show with his friends, drinking an ice-cold beer. Admittedly, when he and his friends first arrived, he was somewhat dubious about their choice for the day out.

Seeing his discomfort, his friend James had laughed. "You're in the horse world now, my friend. We thought you'd like to see what it was all about, plus, there are always pretty ladies in tight jodhpurs to look at!" he quipped. The others burst out laughing, and the tone was set for the rest of the day.

Relaxing and chatting with his friends, David found that he was actually enjoying himself. Then a voice over the loudspeaker system clearly announced, "Coming up next, we have Ellen, from Hollybrook Stables, riding Sundance."

"I know her, she's one of the ladies from the yard," he said to his friends. "Come on, let's go and watch her."

David and his friends made their way through the crowd to the main ring, and then he saw her. His breath caught in his throat at the sight of her, all dressed up in her smart show wear, her strawberry blonde hair tied neatly in a plait that reached all the way down her back. And her horse! He thought Captain was beautiful, but the golden creature she was so elegantly cantering around the ring made Captain look like some sort of peasant horse. Ellen and Sundance were the most captivating things he had ever seen. He couldn't take his eyes off them. He watched in awe as they flew over the enormous jumps, cleanly, confidently and effortlessly. David was completely spellbound.

"What a fantastic, clear round, and well done Ellen and Sundance," the voice echoed through the speakers, as Ellen and Sundance trotted calmly out of the ring to the sound of great applause.

"Shall we go and say well done?" James said with a grin. He'd clearly noticed the way David had been staring at Ellen throughout her round.

Jollied on by his friends, who were keen to meet this spectacular jumping lady, David had little choice but to follow them towards the horse boxes in the hope of finding Ellen and Sundance. He silently prayed that his friends would behave themselves and not embarrass him.

It didn't take long to find them, and as they walked, David watched as she untacked Sundance then started to groom him.

"Hi Ellen," said David, somewhat nervously. "My friends and I saw you jumping and thought we would say hello. You were fantastic!"

David was greeted with a large smile from Ellen. *Phew, hopefully she's forgiven me then,* he thought happily as he returned her smile.

"Wasn't Sundance wonderful?" she replied, gently stroking Sundance's nose.

"Hi, I'm James," said James, reaching out to shake her hand. His other friends followed suit.

"David tells me you're a riding instructor?" James added.

"Yes, I am. I offer lessons to all of the liveries at Hollybrook, and I also have independent clients," Ellen replied.

"Well, that is good news. You see, David here," said James, pointing at David and giving him a wink. "He'd like to learn how to ride, you know, now that he's inherited the horse and everything. What do you think?"

"Inherited?" questioned Ellen, looking at David.

I am going to kill James as soon as Ellen is out of sight, David thought, then tried to compose himself to reply sensibly to Ellen. "Um, yes. He belonged to my mum, she bred him herself. But she passed away a few weeks ago, and I sort of got left with Captain."

Ellen smiled kindly at him. "Of course I'll teach you how to ride him. I can teach you how to look after him as well if you need me to?"

"That would be wonderful! Yes, please," David replied, now feeling relieved that somehow James had managed to sort out both of his problems. Ellen no longer seemed to dislike him, and he would learn how to look after Captain. *Maybe I won't kill James after all,* he mused.

"I have to sort Sundance out now, but I'll see you at the yard soon."

And with that, she turned her attention back to her horse, leaving David filled with excitement and hope as he walked away.

Suzie

"We're going to remove the endotracheal tube from his mouth now," the doctor explained to Suzie.

Suzie just gulped and nodded. Today was the day they were going to try and wake Luke up from the induced coma. She was standing at the back of the cubicle, trying not to get in the way of the doctors and nurses, but also desperate to watch what was going on.

The numerous machines continued to beep, and Emma turned to her and gave her a reassuring smile. It was ghastly watching them remove the large tube that had been placed down Luke's mouth to keep him breathing whilst he was in the coma. The doctor had warned her that it was not a pleasant thing to see, but it had to be done. Once the tube was safely removed, the doctor closely monitored one of the screens, the one which showed that Luke was now breathing on his own.

Luke slowly opened his eyes.

"Luke, can you hear me?" the doctor said. "If you can hear me, raise your hand and lift up your thumb."

The doctor, Emma and Suzie all stared down at Luke's hand. It didn't move at all.

Emma instantly turned to Suzie to reassure her. "It's ok, sometimes it takes a little while."

After an agonizing five minutes, the doctor tried again. "Luke, if you can hear me, raise your hand and lift up your thumb."

A grumble came from Luke, and, with all eyes on his hand, they watched him slowly raise it, then it dropped back down on to the bed.

"That's a good start," announced the doctor. "We never know how long it will take someone to respond, nor the extent of the injury until they wake up. Luke has shown good progress, and since his brain didn't swell up any more whilst being in the coma, I'm starting to feel some positivity for his outcome. I'll be back to check on him later." And the busy doctor turned on his heel and headed into the next-door cubicle.

Emma came over to Suzie and gently put her arm around her. Suzie knew that she must have noticed the tears silently sliding down her face.

"I'd say it's time for a cup of tea, wouldn't you? It's been a stressful day for you."

Suzie nodded as Emma left her to make the tea. *She's so kind,* Suzie thought. She looked down at Luke's handsome face, so still, and she watched him sleep.

Emma returned with the tea, and whilst she continued to check all the monitors, she asked Suzie about Luke and her boys. Happy for the distraction, and to talk about her favourite people, Suzie told Emma about her life with Luke, John, Joseph and their horses, Gilly and Clarissa. As she talked, she thought she saw Luke's hand move. There it was again.

"Emma, he moved!"

Emma and Suzie stared intently at him, and Luke opened his eyes, raised his hand and lifted up his thumb.

Jem

Jem was absolutely exhausted. She felt like she had been in a whirlwind ever since she received that fateful phone call from Suzie. After the mad dash up to the hospital, she and Clare had come home with the boys and Gilly. Clare would be looking after Gilly, and she would take care of the boys, along with Suzie's free-range chickens and cats.

She couldn't understand why she was so tired all the time. The boys weren't any trouble, really. She often had them for sleep overs with her own son, Noah, so they were comfortable in her home. They were at school all day, and for the most part, very well-behaved considering everything that was going on. Even though Suzie and Luke hadn't been together for very long, the boys absolutely adored him, and Jem thought, under the circumstances, they were coping very well.

She was so grateful to her partner, Ben. Every day, to give her a break, he would take them all to the football pitch for extra training to let them burn off any excess energy. They were at the park now, and Jem was too tired to cook, she decided she would get everyone fish and chips as a surprise when they got home from football. She also knew that she would pass the yard to get to the chip shop. She was very much in need of some Pandora time. She grabbed her keys and handbag, climbed into her car and drove to the yard.

"Oh Pandora, I don't know what's wrong with me," she said as she lovingly groomed Pandora's mane. She found the grooming routine very therapeutic and, coupled with the gentle sound of Pandora munching on her hay, it made her finally feel at peace.

With rhythmic strokes of the brush, Jem continued. "The boys are no trouble. In fact, I love having them. Noah is enjoying having them to play with and I love to hear them all laughing and playing together. When they get home from school, I so enjoy it when they all sit around the kitchen table, slurping away at their cups of milk and munching on the cake I've made for them, and hearing about their days. Yes, Pandora, I very much like having a full house. So why am I so tired all the time?"

Pandora looked at her and sighed. Having had her fill of hay, she closed her eyes and snoozed as Jem started to groom her all over her body with Pandora's favourite massage brush.

"Maybe it's just the shock of it all," she told the horse. "Oh, look at the time! I'm sorry, Pandora, but I have to go and get the fish and chips," she announced as she untied Pandora and led her out to her paddock. She saw Clarissa waiting for Pandora at the gate. *They're such good friends,* she smiled to herself. Giving both ponies a farewell stroke, she turned and went down to her car, feeling lighter for having talked things through with Pandora.

Clare

Clare was enjoying her view of the pretty Cornish country lanes from between two grey ears. She had been feeling down that morning, so after yard chores were complete, she decided she was in need of a ride out. She saddled up Ghost, Joe's horse, and plodded down the lane, in the direction of the moors.

She was missing Joe. She tried not to, but her phone call from him last night had been bittersweet. She knew they were all having an amazing time. He was so happy and full of news over the phone, but after hanging up, she felt the emptiness of the house far more profoundly than before his call. Riding Ghost made her feel closer to Joe, and she knew he would be pleased to hear about their ride the next time he called.

She was also worried about Jem. She couldn't put her finger on it, but something just seemed a little bit off with her. Clare got the feeling that she was putting on a bit of a front, and that maybe she was struggling with caring for Suzie's boys. Or maybe she was run down. She wasn't sure, but with a determined nod to herself, she resolved to find out.

And then of course there was Suzie. She was elated to hear the news that Luke was now awake, but Suzie and she both knew that Luke was just at the beginning of the long hard slog of rehabilitation ahead of him, and Suzie would be exhausted with all the support he was going to need.

Clare sighed a deep, heavy sigh. "Oh Ghost, why does life have to be so very unfair sometimes?"

Clare heard her phone bleeping in her pocket. She dug it out and read a message from her horse training contact.

17 hand hunter. Cracking type. Needs putting through his paces to see what he's got. Interested?

She smiled. "Just when life gives you lemons, Ghost, someone offers you some sugar to make lemonade!"

Clare replied straight away.

Definitely, when is he arriving?

Another message bleeped through instantly.

Tomorrow too soon?

This day is getting better and better, Clare thought, pinging off her reply.

Perfect!

Clare and Ghost clip-clopped down the small track that led to the gateway of the moors. Carefully leaning down to unlatch the gate, without dismounting, she maneuvered Ghost through, turned him around and closed the gate behind them. Turning to face the open stretch of moors ahead of them, she soaked in the glorious view and inhaled the sweet scent of the countryside air.

I am so lucky to live in such a wonderful place, she thought gratefully. Feeling happier than she had in a long time, she squeezed Ghost into trot, and knowing what was to come, he happily obliged. Once in trot, she felt his excitement building, anticipating what was to come.

"Ok then boy, are you ready?" she asked him.

His grey ears pricked forward, the barren, open moorland inviting gallivanting and fun. She squeezed him again, and they were off. They made a smooth transition to canter before Ghost opened up to a fast, exhilarating gallop. Clare felt freedom and excitement flooding through her. For Clare, there was no better feeling in the world than being at one with a horse.

Ellen

Ellen was enjoying herself as she, Captain and Pipsqueak tootled around the lanes in a very civilized manner. After seeing David at the show and learning that Captain was an inheritance, she decided she could forgive his lack of compassion on the day of his arrival and agreed to help David learn how to look after him. Captain was proving to be an absolute dream, showing wonderful ground manners every time he was handled. She was sure that David would have no problem with that aspect of his care once he knew what to do.

But in terms of riding, she'd decided that she had better take Captain out for a test ride before allowing David to get onboard. Pipsqueak had invited himself along for the little jolly by point blank refusing to leave Captain's side. Ellen giggled to herself at how smitten Pipsqueak was with him. He literally followed him everywhere. Leading Pipsqueak alongside the gentle giant was proving to be much easier than she had first imagined. His little legs trotted along to keep up with Captain's nicely paced, forward going walk, and both horses were enjoying their little adventure together.

As they plodded along, Ellen let her mind wander back to the day of the show. Sundance had excelled himself in every possible way. She had felt so proud of him, and even a tiny bit smug that she was the one who was riding him. Riley was thrilled when she received the message about how well they had done and loved all the pictures she sent, especially the one of her and Sundance clearing the double spread. The show photographer had captured them at the perfect time, both focused, Sundance's golden ears pricked, mid-air as they effortlessly cleared the jump. She had bought the professional photograph instantly, a special reminder of her perfect day with Sundance.

And then the day got even better! Maybe it was because she was in such a good mood that she didn't have time to think about being cold towards David before he was standing right in front of her with his friends. He seemed different to when she first met him on the yard, more relaxed, less distracted, less edgy. And James. She laughed at how James just bulldozed himself into conversation with her, putting her at ease with the unexpected situation.

She also remembered noticing how good-looking David was, especially standing next to his very ordinary-looking friends. They were nice enough, but David was most definitely the looker in the group, although he didn't seem to know it himself. James was the outgoing cocky one! Closing her eyes, listening to the rhythmic beat of the horses' hooves on the lane, she pictured him. Scuffed brown leather deck shoes, denim jeans, brown belt and a casual blue and white checked shirt, tucked in, showing off his lean figure. Ellen also noticed that his shirt sleeves were rolled up, showing off tanned, strong-looking arms. And the smile he gave her when she agreed to help him! He had smiled the most genuine smile, from his sparkling eyes, with little creases next to them, and his lovely straight teeth on show when his smile broke out.

Thank God I was hanging on to Sundance. It was enough to make me go weak at the knees, she thought, blushing at the memory. She had pretended to be busy with Sundance in order to hide her awkwardness. The feelings she felt for David at that moment were not in the least bit expected, taking her by surprise and knocking her off guard. She felt she'd had to shoo them all away so that she could regain some composure. Clip-clopping home, Ellen decided she was very much looking forward to seeing David again.

Suzie

"Oh Clarissa, how I have missed you," Suzie told her horse, whilst wrapping her arms tightly around her and burying her head in her mane. Breathing in deeply, Suzie inhaled her intoxicating horsey smell, and finally, after an extremely long time, felt at peace.

Luke was doing well; he was no longer in intensive care, having been transferred to the neurological ward where the doctors could oversee his progress. Although improving, he was having problems with his memory, and he got confused and lacked focus. The doctor tried to explain it to her in a way she could understand She was so fed up with all the medical jargon and not really understanding half of the things they told her, that she had been upfront with the doctors and asked for a laymen's explanation.

"His brain is like a jigsaw puzzle," the doctor explained. "All the pieces are there, but they've been muddled up after his fall. It is going to take time for the pieces to go back into the right places of the puzzle. We don't know how long it will take. Each patient is different, and we just have to wait. It will take as long as it needs to take for Luke to put his puzzle back together again."

Suzie finally understood, and she could cope with that. Luke would recover, eventually. She would just have to be patient. Luke's progress had enabled the doctors to allow him to transfer to the hospital in Plymouth, where he would continue with his rehabilitation, and Suzie could finally go home and be with her boys, and Clarissa. How she had missed her darling boys! She would be forever grateful for what Jem had done for her, taking them in and caring for them as if they were her own.

She rested her head against Clarissa, and she felt the tears starting to swell within her again. *Will they ever stop coming?* she thought. "Oh Clarissa," she cried, "it's so very hard, you're the only one I can tell, I just had to come and see you. It's so difficult putting on a brave front for everyone. They all want to hear positive news, and on the whole, it is positive. But what they don't know," she whispered, "is that he can be so mean The doctors warned me that this could happen. The part of his brain that was damaged affects his behaviour and emotions. Apparently, he doesn't know he's doing it, but he can be so snappy with me, so curt with me. It can all get a bit much. Clarissa. I know he doesn't mean to do it, and the doctors said it should reduce over time as he improves, but at the moment I feel like I'm permanently walking on eggshells around him."

With her arms tightly wrapped around her best friend, Suzie cried and cried. All the pent-up feelings that she couldn't explain to anyone else now finally poured out of her, in the safe knowledge that her best friend understood her and would never share her secrets with anyone.

The relief she felt after finally letting go and allowing herself to admit the whole truth out loud to Clarissa left her feeling lighter and stronger than when she arrived. Clarissa filled her with confidence to continue with the long journey laid out before her.

"And that," she said to Clarissa. "That starts with seeing Gilly. I have to see him. It wasn't his fault. I have to face him, and then I can tell Luke that I've seen him, and that he's fit and healthy, just like Clare said." She explained it all to Clarissa with a determined tone to her voice. Saying it out loud to her beloved horse made her believe that she could do it.

She untied Clarissa and turned her out in her paddock with Pandora, then slowly made her way to Gilly's paddock. He looked his usual, gorgeous self, grazing quietly, and at the sound of her voice, he looked up and trotted over to her.

"Oh Gilly," she exclaimed, reaching up and placing her hand on his strong neck. Gilly rested his head on her shoulder and more tears fell. *Surely, there can't be many more in there,* she thought ruefully. After a long, much needed embrace with Gilly, Suzie left the yard, determination and positivity starting to flow through her. Yes, she and Luke were going to get through this.

She drove home, then walked the short walk through the village to collect the boys from school. *Yes,* she thought, *routine. Back to normal, this is what we need, start as we mean to go on.*

"MUM!" she heard her boys call out in unison, as they raced out of the school gates and launched themselves at her in a ginormous hug, almost bowling her over. "You're home!"

David

David was doing his best to concentrate on what Ellen was saying. However, her very tight-fitting black jodhpurs enhanced every single curve and contour of her toned legs and feminine figure, and it was proving very distracting indeed.

"Good job," said Ellen, as David stood back to admire his handiwork. The once mud-caked Captain was now clean and tidy, after David's first grooming lesson.

"Now I'll show you how to pick his feet out," said Ellen, and she ran her hand down Captain's leg, and with a light tug on his fetlock, Captain lifted his hoof up in a very gentlemanly manner.

"Now, with the hoof pick, clean all the mud and dirt out of his hoof using downwards strokes."

David barely heard a word Ellen was saying to him. As she bent over to pick up Captain's foot, he had been given the view of her perfectly-shaped bottom and so far, he had been unable to tear his eyes away from it. *For the love of God, man, get a grip!* he chastised himself. *At least pretend to listen to what she is saying, or you're going to look like a right idiot when you can't answer her questions!*

"Ok, your turn now," Ellen said as she handed him the hoof pick.

David felt eternally grateful to Captain, who lifted his hoof up as soon as he started to run his hand down his leg, preventing David from looking like a complete moron. *Extra carrots for you later,* David thought.

"Well done," Ellen said, smiling at him.

David felt himself glow on the inside after receiving her praise. He didn't know what it was about this horsey lady, but he had never felt anything like it before.

He had an underlying urge to just want to be in her company all the time, and to gently place the lock of hair that seemed to never stay in position, tucked tightly in her plait, in its rightful place. He desperately wanted to brush his fingers over her cheek and tuck the wayward lock behind her ear. *Very, very, bad idea,* he said to himself. Ellen most definitely gave off the air that this was a business deal, part of her job, and although she seemed to have somewhat thawed since their first meeting, he sensed that she had drawn an invisible line and he most definitely was not allowed to cross it. *I'll settle for friends, though,* he thought. *At least I can be around her then, and that's better than nothing.*

Clare

Isaac was Clare's type of horse; big, bold and fearless. He was a 17 hand, dark bay gelding and very accomplished hunter. Although not the most handsome of horses, his willing temperament and agility on the hunting field more than made up for his plain looks and Clare thought he would make someone a wonderful hunter.

His arrival had been uneventful. At ten years old he knew his job. He'd been to many meets in his time, so new yards and new horses were all old news to him, and Clare was pleased that he had settled so quickly. The fun of putting him through his paces started within two days of being on her yard.

After a short lesson in the school to get a feel for him, she had taken him for a gentle walk around the lanes. Isaac took it all in his stride, and Clare felt the typical excitement building in her as Isaac's capabilities and placid personality started to unfold. The real test came when she took him to the local meet, five days after his arrival. What an absolute blast they had. His manners were impeccable. He got on well with any horse he was introduced to, and he was happy to ride at the front, back or right in the middle, at all paces. And boy could he jump. Every hedge, ditch and gate she pointed him at, he sailed right over. Careful, neat and tidy jumping from a super school master.

Clare's contact had been thrilled at her assessment of Isaac and informed her that a buyer was in the pipeline and would be keen to view Isaac as soon as possible.

After a late-night message from her contact the previous evening to inform her that a meeting had been set up for tomorrow, Clare and Isaac were ready and waiting on the yard for a gentleman called Matthew to arrive. Clare had spent a very enjoyable morning grooming and prepping Isaac for his potential buyer, and as she stood back to survey him, she smiled to herself, pleased with his appearance. She saw his ears twitch at the sound of a vehicle heading up the drive.

"This is it, boy," Clare whispered to him. "You are awesome as you are. Just be you." She gave him a quick kiss, then walked down the driveway to meet Matthew.

Clare had always prided herself on being a professional. Her focus was only ever on the horse at hand and doing everything she possibly could to ensure the horse was encouraged to be the best it could be, and matched with the correct owner, enabling the best partnership for them both. Over the many years of her equine career, she had dealt with both men and women, many times over. She never really thought of them as male or female. She always took them on how they behaved around the horses and whose personality matched the best to achieve that perfect relationship between human and horse.

As Matthew stepped out of his car and greeted her with an outstretched hand and friendly smile, Clare felt a jolt within her. On autopilot, she reached out her own hand to shake his on greeting.

And zing! She felt as if an electric current had zapped through her on touching him. *What the hell is the matter with me?* she thought, as she tried to find her tongue in her mouth. She got there in the end.

"Follow me, Isaac is on the yard," she said, the words coming out in a bit of a stutter. Then she swiftly turned away from him to try and gather herself together in the thirty seconds she had for it to take them to reach Isaac.

Matthew introduced himself to Isaac, and while he ran his hands all over him and gave him a thorough going over, Clare stood back and tried to gain control of herself and her somewhat unexpected wayward emotions.

Watching Matthew, she summed him up in her mind. *Early fifties, about six-foot, dark, neatly cropped curly hair, muscular build, and the most handsome man I have ever seen! Never in all my life have I felt an instant attraction to anyone, ever, like I just felt for him. Get a grip of yourself, he's a client, for God's sake!*

"So," said Matthew. "Shall we go riding?"

Jem

Ben had kindly offered to feed Pandora this morning, as yet again, Jem had struggled to wake up and get out of bed. The feeling of lethargy never seemed to leave her at the moment. But Ben had to get to work, and she had to get Noah to school, so she forced herself up and took Noah to school, pushing herself through the daily feeling of wading through sludge.

She was struggling to hide her constant fatigue from Ben. She could feel his concerned look on her more regularly now, He worked so hard, though, and put in so many extra hours as the school football coach. He had already taken over cooking their evening meal, and she didn't want to be even more of a burden to him. She was sure, now that John and Joseph were back with their mum, that she would feel better soon.

She hadn't ridden in weeks; she just didn't feel like she had the energy to do anything other than day-to-day necessities. Pandora was tied up on the yard after receiving her morning feed and daily groom. She was contentedly munching on her hay net as Jem finished up her morning chores.

"You know what, Pandora?" Jem announced. "I feel absolutely terrible anyway. I think we will ride today. At least I can feel miserable with you, doing something I love." And with what little energy she had left in her, she tacked up her horse.

Pandora could sense that she was unwell. She kept to a gentle, steady plod, as Jem rode her around the lanes. Her pace never changed, and Jem started to relax, enjoying the rhythm of her horse. She felt so very grateful to have Pandora, her best friend and confidante, looking after her so well. But as the little horse turned into Hollybrook driveway, Jem sensed that she might have over done it. Emotionally, she felt lighter, and her head was clearer from the fresh countryside air. Her brain slowed, as she lived in the moment of being with Pandora. But physically, she felt absolutely exhausted. *Riding was worth it, though,* she thought. *I'll rest for a couple of hours when I get home.*

Pandora guided herself along the driveway and right up onto the yard, back to where her hay net was tied up waiting for her. With the final remainder of strength left in her, Jem leaned forward, swung her leg behind her and dismounted. Her feet never seemed to find the floor. She just felt herself crumbling to the ground, and with no more energy left in her, she closed her eyes as she lay on the ground, underneath Pandora.

Clare

Matthew was proving to be an excellent riding companion and Clare was thoroughly enjoying his company. It transpired that although Matthew had been a very accomplished rider in his youth, competing in cross country and also being a very keen hunter, after a particularly nasty fall ten years ago at the age of forty-one, he had made the decision to retire from the competitive world and now, he had the very enviable job of working as a buyer.

Clare privately noted to herself that now, at fifty-one, he was just the right age for her. And this was not to mention his accomplishments as a rider. And he was gorgeous to boot! He was very quickly ticking all the correct boxes of her metaphorical 'potential man' prerequisite check list. A list she didn't even know she had, until two hours ago when Matthew first stepped out of his car and zapped her with his charisma. She found him completely intoxicating.

He had some very high-brow clients which enabled him to travel all over the world to meet and greet the owners and trainers of top-class horses. His job was to match the exact criteria of his clients to their required horse.

And you're paid handsomely for your services, no doubt, thought Clare. She sensed a humbleness about him. There was nothing flashy about him, but she noticed that the watch on his wrist was a Rolex, and his car was a Mercedes, albeit an older model, and although there were no logos on show on his clothes, she could tell that they were the type that you just knew cost money because the quality and style was timelessly elegant. She liked him all the more for it. *No one likes a show-off,* she thought. The fact that he was both humble and self-made, a hardworking man, made him even more of a catch in her eyes.

She liked how he was with Isaac, too. *You can tell a lot about a man from how he behaves with animals,* Clare thought, watching his riding style with a professional, critical eye. He had hands as soft as silk and a genuine affection for the horse. He was kind, confident and a brilliant rider. Clare was impressed, and it took a lot to impress Clare.

They finally reached the gate that would give them access to the open moors.

"So," said Clare. "Do want to see how he really rides?"

"Definitely," replied Matthew, giving her his genuine, friendly smile again.

Feeling tongue tied, yet again, in the presence of this intriguing and exciting man, all Clare could do was call out, "Let's go," as she squeezed Ghost into canter, and heard Isaac and Matthew thundering along behind her.

"He's absolutely wonderful, most definitely the horse for my client," Matthew said a little later, as they plodded along the lanes, heading home to Hollybrook.

"I'm so pleased, he truly is a fantastic horse," said Clare as they turned into the driveway and headed on to her yard.

"Oh my gosh…Jem!" Clare shouted, when her eyes fell on Jem sprawled out on the floor underneath Pandora.

Ellen

Ellen was trying to regain some composure and remain professional and level-headed. She was supposed to be David's riding instructor, for goodness' sake! But the more time she spent with him, the harder she was finding it to keep up her distance, and to be her usual calm and collected self.

She was standing in the middle of the school, giving David his first riding lesson after - well, she didn't know how many years, but he said it had been a very long time since he last sat on a horse. It didn't take long for her to notice that he was a natural. Clearly all the years he spent riding with his mother as a child had not been wasted. He was lacking in confidence, but then, Captain was a big horse and years out of the saddle could dent anyone's confidence at the beginning, but his style was good and as the lesson progressed, she felt that his confidence was increasing, the more Captain proved he could be trusted.

She was in a tricky situation. She literally *had* to look at David, all the time – that's what she had to do when giving anyone a lesson. How could she teach without watching her student? But at the same time, she knew, when she was looking at him, that wondering how toned he was, wondering if there was a six pack underneath his navy-blue shirt, was most definitely not what she should be thinking about.

She expected, even hoped, for the sake of her budding little crush, that he would have been awkward, ungainly, once up on Captain, but to her dismay, this was not the case at all. He looked positively gorgeous in his denim jeans, navy blue shirt tucked in, brown belt and brown ankle boots. He did not look in the least bit unsightly - very much the opposite in fact - and now she was struggling to control the feelings that were bubbling up inside her as she watched this handsome man, and his equally handsome horse, trotting elegantly around her in the sand school.

Ellen was brought back into the present from her daydream when she heard David call out, "I think my stirrups might be a bit short, what do you think?"

"Change the rein and trot around me," she replied, and as she watched him ride, she thought, *yep, his stirrups need to go down two holes, which I would have noticed had I not been wondering what he looked like without his shirt on!* She firmly told herself to concentrate – she should at least be giving the impression of being professional!

Aloud, she said, "Bring him back to walk then halt him."

Walking over to David, she placed her hand on his leg to move it forward to adjust his stirrups. As soon as she touched him for the first time, she felt a zing rush right through her. Feeling her cheeks flood with colour, she bent her head to fiddle with the stirrup leathers and drop his stirrups down.

Oh, my word, I'm going to have to touch him again to do the other one, she thought, trying to brace herself against the unaccustomed sensations she felt at being in such close proximity to him. Another zing zapped through her as she touched his other leg, and she could feel more even colour rushing to her cheeks.

"Thank you," said David, and as she looked up at him, she saw his kind eyes twinkling down at her. He held her gaze for just a fraction of a moment too long to be appropriate for a professional relationship between client and instructor.

"You're welcome," she replied shyly, then reluctantly stepped back from Captain and walked back into the middle of the school to continue his lesson.

Suzie

Suzie felt like she and Luke finally had a breakthrough. On arriving at the hospital that morning, she walked into Luke's cubicle to find him sleeping peacefully. In all honesty, she was grateful to find him asleep. His temperamental outbursts were really putting a strain on her. She felt that she couldn't do any more for him; she was both mentally and physically worn out and she had hardly anything more to give to someone who showed very little kindness in return. The doctors continued to explain to her that Luke's temper would improve over time, but that was all they could tell her. How much time was anyone's guess. She would just have to be patient.

After her busy morning of being upbeat and positive for her boys, and getting through the usual morning chaos of breakfast, making packed lunches and finding the ever-missing lost school shoes, her boys were out the door and safely dropped off at school. She managed a quick half an hour with Clarissa to feed and check her and then it was straight to the hospital to see Luke and help him with his rehab. On finding him asleep, she pulled up the chair next to his bed, held his hand in hers, rested her head on the edge of the hospital bed and closed her eyes. She couldn't help herself, she just needed five minutes for a quick rest.

She woke to find Luke gently stroking her face with the back of his hand. It was the first kind gesture he had made towards her since his accident. He had always been affectionate towards her, that was one of the things she loved about him. He was thoughtful and kind and one of her favourite things was snuggling up next to him on the sofa in the evening, with his arm around her, making her feel comforted and loved, as they chatted about their days or read in companionable silence.

Waking to feel his light touch on her brought all of those feelings back and emotions began to flood through her. She felt a lump lodge itself in her throat. She couldn't look at him as her tears silently trickled down her face. She felt his hand gently move under her chin, and as he slowly lifted her chin up to face him, she saw there were tears in his eyes as well.

"I'm so sorry, Suzie," Luke said to her, gesturing with his hand for her to come closer, to carefully lie on the bed next to him so he could place his arms around her and hold her close to him. His lips brushed hers for their first kiss since his accident. She finally sensed a glimmer of her Luke, that he was coming back to her. Lying on the bed next to him, his arms wrapped around her holding her tightly, he whispered, "I will get better, Suzie. I am getting better, and it's all down to you. I couldn't have done any of this without all the support you have given me."

And finally, lying in the comfort of his arms, for the first time since the accident, she slept in contentment.

Clare

"Jem, Jem," Clare called, whilst swiftly dismounting Ghost and racing over to find Jem blinking in bewilderment as to why she was lying on the ground underneath Pandora.

"What happened, are you alright?" asked Clare.

Rolling over to try and sit up, Jem appeared to be attempting to find her bearings. "I don't know what happened," she replied. "Pandora and I went riding, I remember riding right up onto the yard, and now I've woken up on the floor."

Clare carefully manoeuvred the gentle, patient horse out of the way, untacked her, then put Pandora in her stable.

Without being asked, Matthew untacked Ghost and Isaac, turned them out into the closest paddock he could find, then came over to offer his help to Clare and Jem.

"Should we take her to the hospital?" he asked Clare, "She could have bumped her head when she fell? Thank goodness she was still wearing her riding hat. She might have suffered a concussion. It's always better to be safe than sorry in these situations."

Clare nodded in agreement.

Jem tried to protest. Clare sensed she didn't want to be a burden to anyone, but her sixth sense had been telling her that something wasn't quite right with Jem for a few weeks now, so she insisted on taking her to hospital.

"No arguing, Jem. We're taking you to be checked over at the hospital. Would you like me to call Ben?"

"No, please don't. He's at work, there's no need to worry him. I'll call him after I've seen the doctor," replied Jem, slowly managing to haul herself up and sit on the small bale of hay she had conveniently left next to Pandora's stable earlier that morning.

"I'll drive, you can sit in the back and look after Jem," said Matthew. Bending down, he slid his arms around Jem and carefully picked her up and carried her to his car.

Clare just nodded in reply and followed Matthew to his car. Sitting next to Jem on the back seat, her friend resting against her whilst she gently tried to sooth her and reassure her that everything was going to be fine, Clare was secretly wishing Suzie was with them. *She would know all the right things to say. I'm the practical one, I should be driving the car and Suzie should be caring for Jem on the back seat.*

The hospital staff greeted them efficiently and kindly on arrival, then swiftly took Jem away to be examined immediately on hearing she might be concussed after falling off her horse. Clare was told that a nurse would update her on Jem's progress soon.

Matthew is so kind, Clare thought as he quietly sat next to her in the hospital waiting room. He had taken charge of the situation when they first found Jem on the yard and now, even though she assured him that she would be fine on her own, he refused to leave her. Clare felt her eyes begin to close. It was turning out to be an exhausting day, and she was feeling weary from the emotional roller-coaster her life had become over the last few months. She didn't like to admit it, but she was missing Joe terribly, and then there was Suzie. Suzie and Luke were living through every rider's worst nightmare; Luke for personally suffering a terrible accident, and now having to emotionally and physically push his way through gruelling rehabilitation, and also Suzie who had witnessed the tragedy and now was having to support Luke through his ordeal. And now this drama with Jem! It was all getting too much. She couldn't keep her eyes open any longer. She felt her head tilt in sleepiness until it met Matthew's shoulder and rested in comfort. If she didn't feel so terribly tired, she would have been mortified for placing herself into someone else's personal space, but she was too worn out to care about such social niceties, and too tired to move away from him. Matthew didn't move. Instead, she felt his fingers interlock with her own as she rested her hands in her lap, a comforting gesture that she hadn't received from anyone in such a long time. Quietly, side by side, they waited to hear the news about Jem.

David

David was having a somewhat chaotic day. Lara, his secretary, had called in sick that morning. She had never taken a sick day before, always soldiering on, no matter how many times he assured her that he could cope and for her to go home and take the day off. David knew that she must be really poorly to have not come in that morning.

As the day ticked on, he was really starting to appreciate how much she did for him and how efficiently she ran his office. The phone never stopped ringing, his paperwork was scattered about all over the place and his arch nemesis, the photocopier, had packed up. It was beginning to dawn on him why he was banned from using the photocopier and why only Lara was allowed to do the filing. He looked at his watch. It was only midday! Three hours without Lara and the office was falling apart. David made a mental note to show Lara a little bit more appreciation when she returned to the office. *Because clearly, I cannot cope without her!*

David loved his work as a family law solicitor, dealing with people face to face, and negotiating the best results for his clients. He had a way with people that enabled them to feel at ease in his company. They understood that he knew his job and that he would do his best to ensure a fair outcome for all involved. He was well-liked amongst his peers and very highly thought of within his profession, but running his office, without a doubt, was all down to Lara. They worked well together. She respected him enormously for his passionate work ethic and he respected her loyalty and proficiency, even if she was a little bit bossy.

As luck would have it, his twelve thirty appointment was cancelled, giving him chance to regain control of the 'organised chaos' he had unwittingly caused and to pop out to the library to ask if someone could photocopy his paperwork.

David stood back and marvelled at the efficiency of the library assistant. After a few seconds of button pressing, the photocopier emitted a gentle hum, and slowly but surely, his documents copied and slid out of the machine. *How do they do it?* he thought. *Literally every time I touch one of these damned machines, it bleeps madly and breaks!*

David lent against one of the many bookshelves and settled his mind as he waited. After his hectic morning, he was enjoying the peacefulness the library offered. He loved libraries, places filled with books and contented solitude, an escape to anyone's chosen destination for an hour or two when one opened those first pages and entered the magical realm of reading.

Whilst the photocopier whirled away, he allowed his mind to wander, and thoughts of Captain came to him. He smiled to himself as he pictured him, grazing contentedly in his paddock with his funny little shadow glued to his side. Over the past few weeks, David found himself enjoying being with Captain. He actually looked forward to spending time with the horse. Captain gave him the same sense of calm and peace that the library offered him. He experienced a true feeling of tranquillity when listening to the gentle sound of Captain munching on his hay net as he groomed him, and the rhythmic beat of his hooves when he rode, and he liked it. He was starting to understand why his mother had enjoyed being around her horses so much. *They offer a friendship and loyalty that I never knew existed,* David thought.

And Ellen. He smiled at the thought of her. She was making his re-entry into the world of horses very pleasant indeed. Her calm, capable manner enabled David to feel at ease in her company when he was with Captain and her faith in both of them bubbled out of her, giving David the confidence to care for him independently and actually ride him. He wasn't going to kid himself; he and Captain still had a long way to go, but they were definitely on their way to becoming a team, and the more he rode under Ellen's watchful eyes, the more he wanted to ride.

It's almost like an addiction! he mused. He was also starting to understand why all the crazy horsey ladies on the yard were out in the wind, rain and snow, day in, day out, caring for their horses. *Horses are a lifestyle, and I think that the horsey lifestyle has now crept up on me!* Although David was unable to get to the yard every day to care for Captain himself due to his work commitments, he found that when he was working late at night, his thoughts always turned to Captain, wondering how he was and how he had spent his day. He was beginning to notice a pattern. If any free time arose mid-week, his first thought was to go and see the horse. *Yes,* he thought. *I am most definitely turning into one of them...an equestrian!*

The photocopier bleeping in completion of its task brought him out of his daydream and back into the present. He collected his paperwork, offered thanks to the library assistant and headed out of the door.

Then he did a double take. He couldn't believe it! There, on the other side of the street, was Ellen, just stepping out of the bakery.

"Ellen," David called out, crossing the road to catch up with her.

Jem

Jem was sitting in the doctor's office trying to digest the information she had just received.

"I'm what?"

"You're pregnant," the doctor repeated. "About four months. It explains all the fatigue you have been suffering with, coupled with the stress you have been under with the partner of your friend being in a terrible accident, and caring for her children, I'm not surprised you collapsed. You need rest, Jem, and lots of it."

Jem stared blankly at the doctor.

"I'm forty-one, my partner and I made the decision together that we were both happy with just my son Noah. This is a complete surprise."

"Well, geriatric mothers do have to take things a little easier, but you are fit and healthy, so I see no problems ahead of you for your pregnancy."

Geriatric, charming! thought Jem as the shock was beginning to wear off and a little fizz of excitement started to brew in the pit of her belly. A*nother baby! Oh my word, what will they think?* And the fizz quickly turned into panic when she thought about how Noah and Ben would react to her news.

"Congratulations! Please make an appointment to see a midwife as soon as possible," said the doctor, getting from behind his desk to see her out of his office.

She saw Clare and Matthew waiting for her, worry lines etched across their brows, awaiting her fate. She couldn't tell them yet, she needed time to think. Plus, she thought it was only fair that Ben and Noah heard the news first. She collected herself together and slapped a big smile on her face.

"Clare, Matthew, thank you so much for taking such good care of me," she said. "Everything is fine. Exhaustion, that's all. I'm not as young as I used to be. The doctor thinks the extra stress of Suzie and Luke and looking after John and Joseph wore me out. I've been ordered to rest! Other than that, I'm fine."

She saw their faces relax. Clare came to her and wrapped her arms around her, holding her tightly.

"Phew! You had us worried for a moment. Let's take you home," said Clare.

On Jem's insistence, Matthew took her to the yard. Her car was still there, and it would be much easier for her to drive the five minutes home herself, and secretly, she needed to see Pandora. She could feel Clare and Matthew's eyes on her from the kitchen window as she unlatched the stable door and slipped inside. Pandora, always pleased to see her mistress, stopped munching on her hay and looked at Jem with her kind eyes. When Jem stood directly in front of her, she slowly lowered her nose and gently sniffed her belly.

"You know, don't you girl," said Jem, stroking Pandora's large roman nose. "No riding until baby is here," she told Pandora with a tinge of sadness in her voice. "But Noah can ride you, and I'll still be here every day and continue to keep you in the manner you are accustomed to," she giggled to her little horse. "I worry about Noah. He took the divorce from his father so well, and then adjusted from Ben simply being his adored football coach, to being the man I fell in love with, who is now firmly part of our family. I'm so proud of the way he has coped with everything, I don't want to do anything that might upset him. But it's not like I can hide it from him. I'll have to explain that a new baby won't change the way I feel about him. He will always be my golden boy."

She felt better having confided in Pandora. She always made anything and everything seem achievable. In Pandora's company, she felt like a blanket of calm was placed around her, and as her little horse listened intently to the trials and tribulations of her life, Jem felt positivity begin to simmer inside her. "You really are the best tonic in the world," she said, leaning her head against Pandora's and resting her hand on the mares neck. "My therapist!" She dropped a kiss on Pandora's nose. She clipped on Pandora's lead rope, led her out of the stable and up to her paddock. Clarissa looked up as soon as she saw her friend. Trotting over to the gateway, she waited for Jem to turn Pandora out, and Jem watched the two horses groom each other with affection after their few hours of separation.

She smiled to herself, and after waving to Clare through the kitchen window, she climbed into her car and headed home.

Clare

It was dawning on Clare what a truly lovely man Matthew was, especially since learning that he had chosen to stay at the hospital and support her whilst waiting for news about Jem, instead of catching his flight to France to meet with one of his highbrow clients. On their parting, a week ago, he asked if she would like to go out for dinner with him when he returned. She felt herself blush like a teenager, secretly thrilled that he might be feeling the electric chemistry she felt when she was in his company.

It had been a long week. Clare tried to keep herself busy with the horses. When she rode, she lost herself in the moment of being with the horse. Working in partnership brought out the best of both of them. But as soon as she climbed out of the saddle, boom! Matthew was back in her thoughts. She had also spent a secretive two hours shopping for something new to wear. Having not been on a date in what felt like centuries, her wardrobe was filled with work yard clothes and good yard clothes, the latter being ones she felt she could wear to complete her yard chores and still deem herself respectable to pop into town for running errands or meet up with a friend for lunch, but not appropriate for a date. She spent an absolute fortune, but as she placed all the glossy carrier bags into the boot of the car after her fruitful trip, she felt ready to tackle the date issue.

Clare surveyed herself as she stood in front of the mirror, wearing her new Marks and Spencer underwear. Although now in her mid-forties, a life spent working physically hard left her with a slim toned figure. *Not bad*, she thought, as she turned to look at herself from a different angle. *Not great, but not bad either!* Pleased with her bra and knickers matching set in navy blue with pale pink roses on them, she slipped on her new navy blue, figure hugging, knee-length dress and teamed it with her favourite pale pink scarf. It had been her mother's, and she didn't wear it very often for fear of losing it, but tonight, she felt it lifted her plain-coloured dress and gave her confidence as she twirled in front of the mirror. She then opted for low-heeled navy-blue court shoes, smart and elegant. Clare had never been one for high heels and going from yard boots to high heels was a risk. She did not want to fall flat on her face in front of Matthew! A spritz of her favourite perfume and a slick of lip gloss, and she was ready. *Just in time,* she thought, hearing his car pull up outside her house.

Zing...went her body as soon as she opened the door and saw him. "Hi, Matthew."

"You look wonderful," he replied. "Are you ready?"

Tongue tied, yet again, in Matthew's presence, all she could do was nod, and follow him to his car.

Clare finally started to relax when Matthew moved his foot under the table and accidentally knocked hers, but rather than moving away, he looked at her for a brief second, a cautious smile on his face, and left his foot gently resting against her own. The conversation began to flow more naturally after that, as if they both now understood their present situation.

Matthew was proving to be excellent company again. Clare listened attentively as he animatedly described some of his more eccentric clients; the lord in Scotland who insisted on strawberry cheesecake for breakfast every morning, and the client he had just been to visit in France, for whom every horse had to be bay. No matter how many times he found a suitable horse in every other way for her, it would not be considered unless it was bay. And there was one other client that Clare found utterly hilarious, who drove Shetlands. Matthew described the assortment of pedigree mischief makers he owned, just like Pipsqueak, in exceptional detail, leaving Clare crying with laughter at the antics the Shetlands and their owner got up to.

"One time, at a prestigious show, he hitched his pair of ponies up to the little cart to give them a warm-up before their class, and the little blighters took off like miniature freight trains, charging through all of the tents, weaving past all of the tables and goods for sale. My client just raised his cap, calling out, "Excuse us, don't mind us!" They left a trail of destruction behind them without a care in the world!"

Clare felt disappointment shroud her on hearing Matthews' next comment. "I'm actually flying to Dubai in two days to meet a sheik client to discuss racehorses. I'll be gone for ten days."

Clare forced herself to return his smile. "How exciting," she said, in the perkiest voice she could manage.

"I was hoping, when I return, that I could see you again? I know Isaac will be collected and taken to his new owner in Surrey before my return, but maybe we could meet in a non-business-related capacity?" Matthew tentatively enquired.

Clare smiled shyly at him, her anticipation and excitement pausing the disappointment she had previously felt. "I'd like that. I'd like that very much."

Matthew, proving once again his gentlemanly manners, opened the car door for her on returning her to her home, and walked her to her door.

"I've had a wonderful evening, Clare." He leaned towards her and gently placed a kiss on her cheek.

Breathing in his subtle, masculine aftershave, Clare closed her eyes and returned his affectionate gesture and kissed him on his cheek.

"So have I, thank you," she replied.

Ellen

"You are the porkiest of porky ponies! You are coming with me to do some much needed exercise," Ellen told the reluctant Pipsqueak. "We'll be gone for an hour. I promise you, Captain will still be here when we get back. Now don't be so needy, it doesn't suit you." Ellen firmly clipped the lead rope onto his headcollar and led him away from Captain and onto the yard.

Ellen felt Sundance glare at her when he realised that the munchkin would be joining them for their ride. "Don't you start! You're supposed to be teaching the little rascal how a horse should behave," Ellen reminded him, kissing his nose before climbing into his saddle. "Come on boys, let's go riding."

She planned to school Sundance that morning but, unusually for her, she was lacking focus and concentration. Instead, she decided she needed time to think, to get a hold of the jumbled-up emotions she seemed to be feeling at the moment. A relaxing hack would do the trick. She did her best thinking when she was alone, with only horses for company.

It didn't take long for Sundance and Pipsqueak to fall into a steady pace together, Pipsqueak's little legs skipping along beside them, taking in all his surroundings.

"See, I told you it wouldn't be so bad. We all know how nosy you are!" Ellen said to the happy little pony. She settled into Sundance's saddle. He was taking his responsibility of showing Pipsqueak how to be a well-behaved horse very seriously, so Ellen could relax and turn her thoughts to David, a subject on which in-depth thought was most definitely needed.

She had been so surprised to bump into him last week in town. It was so out of context that it took her a couple of seconds to work out that the handsome man, wearing charcoal grey suit trousers, a pristine white shirt, and matching charcoal grey waistcoat, was David. Having only seen him in his casual yard clothes, she was quite taken back seeing him dressed just like how she imagined a solicitor might look. She liked his style, especially the quirky waistcoat. You didn't see many men in their thirties wearing one of those these days, but somehow, he pulled it off, looking effortlessly masculine and understatedly stylish.

Ellen had been secretly thrilled when David invited her back to his office to have lunch together. It was always exciting to step into someone else's world, and his office didn't disappoint. Bookshelves lined his walls, jam-packed to the point that overspill books were stacked up neatly, piled high beside his olde-worlde mahogany desk. *Just like out of the movies,* Ellen thought. His desk was full of organised piles of paperwork, with one lone photograph on it. A beautiful Irish draft mare and her foal, with an attractive woman beaming at the camera, with one arm casually draped over the mare.

David caught her looking at the photo. "That's Captain as a foal," he explained. "With his mother, Daisy Mae, and my mum."

Ellen was quick to note that there was only one chair available, the chair behind the desk. Both of the clients' chairs were piled up with higgledy-piggledy paperwork, looking most out of place in an otherwise organised office.

"No, don't worry, I'll sit on the floor," Ellen told David, as he moved to make space on the chair for her.

Ellen settled down on the lush, burgundy carpet.

"My secretary is off sick," David said, pointing to the chairs. "Organised chaos," he added with a rueful smile.

Ellen felt her heart skip a beat when David sat down next to her, so close to her that he was most definitely in her personal space, but she didn't move away. As they sat in companionable silence, munching on their Cornish pasties, Ellen felt an agreed acknowledgment pass through them. They both knew they were on the cusp of stepping beyond the professional relationship of instructor and client and moving towards something else.

"And that, Sundance, is where my predicament lies," Ellen said out loud to the horse, as they rode along together. "What do I do now? I'm in unchartered territory, I have never crossed my professional line before. As soon as I finished my pasty, I made my excuses and hot footed it out of there. I needed time to think, you know, about how I feel about him and everything. He is just so lovely. Oh goodness, what if I make a fool of myself? Sundance, what do you think I should do?"

Sundance put his nose in the air and snorted, as they continued to plod along the country lanes. "Well, that was helpful," Ellen replied, her voice laced with sarcasm.

Sundance suddenly slowed, and then stopped. "What's up?" Ellen asked him, then after a brief pause, he continued on his way. He did it again, this time with a slightly longer pause.

"Oh, I get it! I should wait for him to make the first move! Thanks Sundance, I knew you'd know what to do."

Suzie

Suzie felt a lump form in her throat as she stood back and watched Luke and Gilly. The handsome gelding grazed peacefully as Luke approached his paddock. On hearing Luke call out his name, Gilly froze, his magnificent body poised and alert. Ears pricked forward, he turned his elegant head towards the direction of the voice he knew so well. Luke opened the field gate and stepped inside, and Gilly bolted, running in a flat-out gallop across his paddock to greet his friend, who was standing quietly waiting for him. Gilly slammed his breaks on, and with perfect timing, three feet from Luke, he skidded to a halt.

Suzie could no longer hold back her tears as she watched Luke embrace his horse for the first time in five months. His arms snaked around Gilly's neck and he buried his face in his mane, and the huge gelding rested his head on Luke's shoulder. The two friends, standing in silence, were so very grateful to be together again.

Luke beckoned Suzie over to join him in the paddock with Gilly. "I couldn't have done this without you, Suzie," he said, inviting her to join in a three-way hug with Gilly. "I can't believe how lucky I am to be here with you and Gilly."

Suzie rested her head on Luke's shoulder, enjoying every moment of Luke and Gilly's reunion, until she heard Luke mutter to Gilly, "So old boy, shall we go riding? It's been five months; do you think we can both remember what we're supposed to do?"

Suzie felt panic sweep through her. "Wait a minute," she blurted out. "Did the doctor say you could ride? You said we were just coming to see Gilly; you didn't mention riding him. He hasn't been ridden since your accident. I don't think it's a good idea."

Luke turned to face her. "Steady on, Suze," he replied. "I didn't mean right this second. But soon. I'll speak to my doctor first if you want me to, but no matter what he says, I will ride Gilly again." Wrapping her up in his arms, he whispered, "it's going to be ok; everything will be fine. Think of you and Clarissa, I would never come between you both, I would never do anything to prevent you from doing what you wanted to do with her."

Clarissa isn't the size of a small bus, Clarissa isn't a high-octane jumping machine, Clarissa and I can't reach the dazzling speed you and Gilly do, and I haven't just spent five months in hospital and rehab! she thought to herself. But seeing the steely determination in his eyes, she thought it best to keep her opinions to herself. Deep down, she also knew that he was right. He would never come between her and Clarissa. He had painstakingly helped her with jumping, albeit two foot high, but he had encouraged and supported them, and not once did he tell her she couldn't do it. Aloud, she said, "I'll come with you to see the doctor. I'd like to hear for myself what he has to say."

"Ok, agreed," Luke replied. "Now, let's go and get the boys from school. I think we should have pizza for dinner tonight!"

Clare

Clare had been as tactful as she could be when Suzie came to her for advice the previous day. She understood the anxiety Suzie must be feeling, but she also knew that if Luke wanted to start riding again, then that is exactly what he must do. The doctor has given him the all clear and he would not have done that unless he was absolutely certain Luke was fit enough to ride. After assuring her that Luke was a professional, capable rider, and that Gilly was a sensible, trustworthy horse who would walk through fire for Luke, Suzie began to calm down about the whole situation. Then Clare went on to explain that she couldn't stop him even if she wanted to. It would be better to support him rather than fall out with him about it. And that was the moment when she had offered to take Gilly on a trial hack. That way she could get any potential kinks out of him after his five-month break, before Luke rode him.

Clare tightened up the girth. "It's back to work, my friend. Let's go!" Then she climbed into the saddle and directed Gilly down the drive for a plod around the lanes. Clare thought back to the bad-mannered horse her client sent her to train last year. *What a difference the right owner makes*, she thought, as Gilly clip-clopped along in a very gentlemanly fashion. "You and Luke were just made for each other," she told him, breathing in the fresh countryside air with a smile on her face. "I reckon you and Luke are a right pair of fearless hooligans when left to your own devices," she chuckled to Gilly, recalling the many stories Luke had told her about his and Gilly's crazy hacks. The perfect partnership in the jumping ring; steady, focused, and perfect precision. But Luke would often tell her that out on their own, on a hack, his speed and agility was matched by no other horse.

Clare stopped at the crossroads. Left for the lane route home, or right for the route home with the old farm track they sometimes used as the canter track. She only planned on a gentle hack. *But surely a quick blast wouldn't be too much for the unfit horse?* she mused, turning right. She felt Gilly build with anticipation. She had ridden him here many times before when training him. A gentle squeeze brought him into a forward going trot. *I'm doing Luke a favour,* she told herself. *It's best to check he hasn't reverted back to his naughty ways of bucking into canter,* she justified to herself, and with another squeeze, they were off. Clare had forgotten just how quick Gilly was. There was no bucking, no bad manners, just a smooth transition from trot to canter, and a fast canter at that. Buzzing with his speed and well-mannered response to her cues, she gave a gentle squeeze on his reins, and he slowed down to trot. "Better not over-do it," she said to the horse, bringing him down to a nice forward paced walk to cool him off for the short walk home. "I could not be prouder of you," she said to Gilly, affectionately patting his neck in praise. "And I can honestly tell Suzie that Luke will be absolutely fine to start riding you again."

Clare turned Gilly into her driveway and felt her mobile phone buzz in her pocket. Pressing open message, she read:

Matthew: Miss you x

Grinning from ear to ear, she let go of Gilly's reins and replied:

Miss you too x

David

David pulled into Hollybrook stables driveway and saw a flash of gold out of the corner of his eye. Parking his car, he climbed out and turned to face the sand school. Mesmerized, he watched Ellen and Sundance launching themselves over a huge jump. He stared, transfixed, as they cantered towards the next jump, concentration cemented on Ellen's face, Sundance focused and listening to the cues from his rider, and together, they flew. It was like watching an elegant dance, two partners working together in perfect harmony.

"Am I late or are you early?" Ellen called out to him, trotting Sundance over to the gate.

"I'm early," David replied. "I thought I would give myself plenty of time to get Captain ready before our lesson."

"Ok, you get Captain from his paddock, and I'll cool Sundance down," Ellen said, beaming down at him from her golden Pegasus-like horse. Her cheeks were rosy from the exertion of riding and David noted there was a twinkle in her eyes. He struggled to tear himself away from her. He found her positively intoxicating.

David and Captain were waiting on the yard for Ellen to return from turning Sundance out into his paddock. With them was an unwelcome visitor. David glared at the little pony.

"And now I'm going to have to explain to Ellen that I can't even manage a little midget like you when asked to catch my own horse," he told Pipsqueak, who had rudely shoved past him and Captain and mischievously trotted himself down to the yard. Enjoying his newfound freedom, he was busy helping himself to more of the winter hay supply, with no concern for David's dented ego at all.

Ellen joined David on the yard, leading Ghost behind her. David winced and then realised that she had mistaken his strained look as uneasiness at being in the proximity of such a large gelding.

"Don't worry, he's super friendly. His name is Ghost. He's going to be joining us for your lesson today."

"Um, it's not that," David mumbled, as a bang, swiftly followed by a crashing noise, came from the feed room. "I've got myself into a bit of a situation," he admitted, with a little bit of colour creeping over his face in embarrassment.

To further his shame, Ellen burst out laughing and before asking any more questions, hollered, "Pipsqueak, get out here right now!"

Naughty Pipsqueak poked his nose around the door of the feed room, and fixing his innocent brown eyes on Ellen, David swore he could see a smirk on the mischief maker's face.

"He slipped out when I opened the gate to bring Captain in. I'm so sorry! I'll help you tidy everything up."

"Don't worry, he does it to all of us!" Ellen replied, still laughing. "Before Captain arrived, he was Mr Houdini! We all spent far too many hours chasing after the little monster! But since Captain is his designated new best friend, he's been much better behaved. He probably doesn't want to be left behind."

She turned her attention to Pipsqueak. "So, my little porky pony, you can join us on our ride. Let's see if we can shift a little bit of fat off you after your gluttonous bout in the feed room."

David sighed in relief on hearing that Pipsqueak was naughty for everyone, not just him, and felt his confidence beginning to return.

David busied himself grooming and tacking up Captain, whilst Ellen prepared

Ghost and Pipsqueak. "I thought today we could hack out to the canter track. It's the safest place for you to have your first canter out of the school."

"Brilliant," replied David. He had been waiting patiently for Ellen to decide when she felt he would be ready for a good run. Cantering in the school was getting boring now that he had got the hang of it.

They mounted their horses, and with little Pipsqueak skipping alongside Ghost, they headed down the drive.

"Sundance is a beautiful horse," David remarked, as they chatted away, enjoying each other's company in the peaceful countryside.

"Indeed, he is, although he's not mine. He belongs to Riley, Clare's son's girlfriend. She'll be home soon. I guess I'll have to find another horse to ride then," she replied ruefully. "Although, I doubt I'll find a horse as wonderful as Sundance."

David smiled kindly at her. He could see how much Sundance meant to her. "Well, you can always borrow Captain."

David felt tingles when she smiled her genuine smile at him., "Thank you, that's very kind of you," she replied. "We're here now, are you ready?"

"Very much so," David replied, excitement bubbling up inside him.

Ellen took the lead down the single file track, turning to face him. "Let's go!" she called.

David felt free for the first time in a long time as Captain cantered steadily up the track, and little Pipsqueak zoomed along beside Ghost. He was touched that Ellen kept turning around to check that he was ok. *No doubt checking that Captain and I have not parted company!* he chuckled to himself. He knew it was because of Ellen that he had found his confidence to ride again, and that she was the one who had initiated the friendship, the partnership, that he and Captain were tentatively forming together, and for that, he was most grateful to her. All too soon, Ellen started to slow Ghost and Pipsqueak, and it was over. They had run the length of the farm track, and their horses reverted to plodding along again as soon as they were back on the country lane.

"Fun?" Ellen enquired, once he and Captain were riding up alongside her.

"Absolutely," David replied.

"You're very lucky. Captain is a fabulous horse," Ellen said, casting an admiring eye over his horse.

They chatted companionably for the rest of the ride home. Whilst untacking and grooming down their horses, David started to feel deflated knowing that they would be parting company soon, and he was going to miss her. He enjoyed her company and when he wasn't with her, he often caught himself thinking of her, counting down the days until his next riding lesson.

"You did brilliantly," Ellen said. "I'm off to my next client now but I'll see you next week for your lesson."

Without thinking, or he might have stopped himself, he gently put his hands on Ellen's arms, lent forward and placed a kiss on her cheek "Thank you for today," he replied. "I'm looking forward to seeing you next week,"

Ellen slowly raised her head, looked into his eyes and smiled. "I'm looking forward to seeing you again too." Then she was gone.

David exhaled as he watched her get into her car, wave at him, then drive away. *Well, I think that went well,* he thought.

Jem

Jem felt as ready as she would ever be, sitting at the kitchen table waiting for Ben to return with Noah from football practice. The table was laid to indicate that a special family meal was in order; the special 'family occasion' cream crockery with dainty yellow and baby blue flowers adorned the table, along with candles and the delicious smell of roast beef with all the trimmings wafted over from the oven. Several bottles of the brand of beer that Ben liked the most were chilling in the fridge and chocolate brownies, Noah's favourite, were cooling on the wire rack for pudding.

Jem didn't really know why she hadn't told Ben and Noah about the pregnancy straight away. When they'd asked her how she was on her return from hospital, she'd simply replied, "It's just exhaustion from doing too much. I'm not as young as I used to be, the doctor said I just need to rest." She didn't know why those words had popped out, instead of the truth, but they'd both accepted her response without question. And they had both been fussing over her and ensuring her every need was met. She smiled at the thought of how lucky she was to have such a caring family.

Jem had been proactive since learning of her pregnancy. The doctor calling her geriatric had worried her, so she had contacted the midwife straight away, and been in luck. A cancellation meant that she had been able to have her first scan the day before, just seven days after her hospital visit. Emotion welled up inside her on seeing her little baby on the screen for the first time, and the nurse announced him or her to be fit and healthy. She smiled smugly to herself. She may be old, but she was still managing to grow a perfectly healthy baby. And that was the moment she knew it was time to tell her boys. She wanted them to share in her excitement now that she knew all was well with the new member of their family.

She had told Ben that evening. She waited until Noah was fast asleep and once she and Ben were settled in bed, she asked Ben to close his eye and hold his hand out. Carefully placing her scan photo into his hand, she then told him to open them. Watching the open delight shine across his face as his eyes scanned the picture, told her all she needed to know. Ben was equally thrilled about the baby as she was.

"You're happy?" she enquired.

"I'm over the moon. This is the best news ever. I can't believe it, I'm going to be a dad!" said Ben, enveloping her in his arms.

She heard them chatting football talk as they noisily came through the front door and dropped their football kits to the ground before bursting into the kitchen.

"Something smells delicious," remarked Ben, dropping a kiss on Jem's forehead.

"Chocolate brownies!" exclaimed Noah. "Can I have one?"

"After dinner," laughed Jem. "Wash up, boys, I'm serving up now."

"Why are we using the fancy plates?" Noah asked as he seated himself at the table and started to load his plate with roast potatoes and Yorkshire puddings.

"I have news," Jem tentatively told him. "Some very good news."

Noah stared at her. *Well, I've got his attention now,* she thought. *Time to tell him the truth.*

"I'm going to have a baby!" Jem blurted out, producing her precious scan photograph and cautiously handed it to him.

"A baby?" Noah said, taking the photo and scrunching his eyes as he tried to work out what the picture was. "Does that mean I'm going to be like John and have a little brother?"

"It means you're going to be a big brother like John, but not necessarily have a little brother like Joseph. You might get a little sister," Jem explained, pointing to the picture and carefully drawing her finger over it to show the outline of the baby.

"This is great news," Noah said, smiling at her. "I'm not going to be on my own anymore, I'll have someone to play with all the time."

Jem felt like a weight had been lifted with Noah being so enthusiastic about becoming a big brother.

Ben stood up from the table and opened out his arms. "Come here you two, family hug time!"

As Noah squeezed in between Jem and Ben, she felt two pairs of arms wrap around her and hold her tight. Jem had never felt so much happiness and contentedness in all of her life.

Suzie

Suzie was feeling apprehensive, but she knew she couldn't put it off any longer, so she reluctantly agreed to Luke riding Gilly today, provided that she and Clarissa went along with them. The horses were tacked up and Luke was busy packing their picnic into Gilly's saddle bags.

"Are you ready?" Luke asked her, bringing her out of her worry-filled thoughts.

I'm not going to be a spoil sport and ruin this for Luke, he has been so looking forward to this, she firmly told herself. Turning to face Luke, she tried her best to sound chirpy. "Yes, Clarissa and I are ready," she replied.

Suzie had to admit, Luke was staying true to his word, and their gentle hack was turning out to be just that. The horses clip-clopped along at a gentle pace, the air was calm and riding alongside Luke again, she could feel the fizz of attraction for him that she always felt when watching him ride. He was so calm and relaxed in the saddle, oozing confidence. *And so handsome,* she thought. She always noticed other women looking at Gilly and Luke at shows, and in her opinion, she couldn't blame them, Gilly and Luke were the best-looking horse and rider team wherever they went, and she always felt so smug when Luke dismounted after his class and scooped her up in his arms in celebration. Gilly and Luke never left a show without being in the ribbons.

"This looks like a nice spot," Luke announced, pointing to a large open field that had a pretty little stream running through it. "The horses can have a drink and we can sit on the riverbank for our picnic."

"It's perfect," Suzie agreed, following Luke into the field.

Luke led the horses to the water for them to quench their thirst whilst Suzie laid out the blanket and picnic. They settled down to enjoy the fresh sandwiches and Victoria sponge cake Suzie made that morning.

After a while, Luke looked at her intently. "You made me better, you know that don't you Suze?" he said. "So many times, I just wanted to give up. The frustration would eat away at me, the dark thoughts that I would never be the same again, that I wouldn't be the man I was before my accident. Some days I just didn't want to face the long hard therapy sessions I knew were ahead of me. But then I would think of you, and the support you gave me, every single day. Even the days when I was miserable and full of self-pity. The days when I was downright unpleasant to you and didn't deserve your patience and kindness. I wanted to get better for you, I would think about riding with you, you and me riding Clarissa and Gilly, not the shows or the hard training, just lazy rides like we're doing today. And your boys, playing football in the park with them, having wrestling matches with them and competing in who can eat the most ice cream before brain freeze kicks in," he said, laughing. "I want you know that I appreciate everything that you have done for me."

Suzie felt tears spring to her eyes as Luke voiced all the things she had dreamed he would say to her during the depths of her own pain after his accident. She often felt shame for her own self-pity during those times, but no one ever tells you how hard it is for the person enduring the repercussions of a terrible accident, looking on from the outside. Apart from Clarissa, she had never breathed a word to anyone about the hurt she had experienced during the past five months. She felt like she would have been cheating Luke out of the attention and support he needed, if their friends had given her the support instead.

Luke tenderly placed his hand on her face and wiped her tears away with his thumb. "I'm better now, everything is going to be fine," he said, smiling at her. He pulled her into his arms and affectionately kissed the top of her head, holding her close to him. "Suzie, will you marry me?"

Pulling away from his tight embrace, Suzie looked at him, straight into his eyes.

"Yes, I would love to marry you," she replied, and then, leaning into him, Suzie placed both hands on either side of his face and kissed him.

Sitting side by side, with Luke's arm around her, watching their horses graze, Suzie felt overwhelmed with gratitude that after everything they endured, this perfect day together had been waiting for them. Closing her eyes, she rested her head on Luke's shoulder, allowing herself to finally feel excited about what the future would hold for them.

Ellen

Ellen woke with a heavy heart. Riley was coming home tomorrow, so today was her last day with Sundance. It was her last chance to ride the beautiful golden horse she had fallen so in love with. She held back the tears as she pushed off her duvet and climbed out of bed. She had always known that this day would come, and she was excited about seeing her friend again. She refused to allow herself to wallow in self-pity. Her last day with Sundance would not be filled with sadness. Plus, she was seeing David today. The thought of David brought a little smile to her face, encouraging her to feel a little bit more positive about the day ahead.

No matter how hard she tried, though, she couldn't dislodge the lump that wedged itself in her throat as soon as she saw Sundance. She was pleased she had arrived early. She wanted time on her own with Sundance before David arrived. Grooming his silky mane, she could bear it no longer. Wrapping her arms around her golden friend, she finally let go and cried. Time stood still as she silently sobbed into Sundance's warm, comforting neck, mentally reliving all the wonderful times they spent together.

"I'll still see you," she whispered into his neck. "You just won't be mine anymore, but Riley will be back." Sundance nickered at the sound of Riley's name. "I know, she's your human. You've missed her, haven't you boy?" Ellen knew how much Sundance and Riley meant to each other, and she was grateful to have been given the opportunity to get to know such a wonderful horse, but now it was time to return him to his rightful owner.

Ellen felt better after letting it all out. Not one for being overly emotional when it came to human relationships, Ellen couldn't help herself when it came to horses. She felt it was much easier to be herself with them and share her thoughts with them more than any human friend. *Although,* she mused, *David is definitely becoming someone I feel I could trust, and someone I can be myself with.*

On cue, she heard David's car turn into the driveway and trundle up to the carpark. Swiftly drying her eyes, she turned to Sundance. "How do I look? I hope I don't look like an emotional wreck!" Sundance snuffled her neck with his nose, tickling her so she burst out laughing. "You have the answer for everything, don't you," she giggled, kissing him on his nose.

"How do you feel about having your first ride on the moors?" she asked David as soon as he walked onto the yard.

"Sounds great fun, I'm in!" replied David. "I'll get Captain ready."

David was proving to be a great riding companion. He seemed to pick up on her instructions quickly and over the last six months, his riding had improved tenfold. Ellen felt secretly proud of the progress David and Captain had made together, and now they were out of the beginner stages, she felt that the fun was just about to start. Blasting around on the moors or charging along the woodland tracks like a loon was great fun, but only if one was a confident capable rider, and she was hoping, if David competently managed a steady canter across the open moors today, that they would have lots of adventurous riding hacks ahead of them. *Yikes,* she thought, *getting ahead of myself there, I haven't even asked him if that's what he would like to do!*

"Are you ok?" David enquired, as they walked along the lane, side by side.

"Sorry, I was miles away. I was thinking about taking you to the woods one day. There are lots of great canter tracks there if you wanted to go?" she asked shyly.

"Sounds great," he replied enthusiastically.

"We're here now," Ellen announced. "Once we go through this gateway, we're on the moors. Keep Captain behind me at all times, ok?"

"Will do," David said, positioning Captain a few feet behind Sundance.

"Isn't the view amazing?" Ellen said, looking across the open moorland before them.

"Beautiful, especially seeing it through two grey ears!" David replied.

"Ready?" Ellen asked.

David nodded in reply as Ellen pushed Sundance into a few strides of trot, and then they were off. Ellen embraced the unequalled sensation of freedom she felt when Sundance carried her at high speeds across open ground. Coupled with the sound of the thundering hooves beneath her, there was no other feeling like it.

She was lost to the moment, riding fast and free spiritedly, exhilaration circulating through her veins. Her last ride with Sundance. With a jolt, she remembered David. *Oh my god, David,* she thought, turning around. She saw Captain, keeping up effortlessly behind her, and David grinning from ear to ear. *Well,* she thought, *I reckon David and Captain are ready to blast around the woods with me after that!* She was utterly thrilled with David's riding capabilities.

She steadied Sundance and gently slowed him to walk. He was breathing hard after his long, exhausting run.

David, slightly breathless asked, "Can Captain and I ride alongside you again now?"

She turned to David. "Of course, come on up. Did you have fun?"

"The most fun I've had in a very long time! Thank you, Ellen."

Leaving the moors and joining the lane for home, Ellen felt her elation swiftly turn to deflation, as she realised that it was nearly all over. Her time with

Sundance would very soon be coming to an end. The lump in her throat that fleetingly vanished during her run over the moors was back, and a solitary tear silently slipped down her cheek.

Ellen was lost within her own thoughts for the rest of the ride home, and in what felt like no time at all, they arrived back at the yard. After dismounting, she led Sundance in silence up to the yard, and another unintended tear rolled out.

David's voice penetrated through her thoughts. "Are you ok, Ellen? You were very quiet on the way home."

She instantly felt rude for having been so quiet, and intended to put a brave face on it, but when she turned to face him, the look on his face showed her that she had not managed to hide her feelings from him.

In two strides, he covered the ground between them and wrapped his arms around her. "What's wrong?" he asked. "You can tell me; I might be able to help."

Ellen felt herself relax into his arms, and as she sobbed inelegantly into his shoulder, she blurted out how upset she was about Sundance. She explained to him how devastated she felt to be returning a horse that wasn't even hers to begin with.

"Just out of curiosity, why don't you have your own horse? I've often wondered. Maybe it's time for you to make the investment now. Then you'll never have to go through the heartbreak of giving one back to its rightful owner," David quietly suggested.

Ellen felt herself nodding into his shoulder, "I've spent so many years training to become a riding instructor, and so many years working with other people's horses, gaining experience with as many different types of horses as possible to help me progress as a horse trainer. It's taken me many years to build my coaching and training business and I just haven't felt like I've had the time to dedicate to a horse of my own. I loaned a horse a couple of years ago from a friend when she was pregnant, but once the baby was six months old, she was ready to have her horse returned and I told myself it was for the best. I needed to concentrate on continuing to build my business. But now, maybe you're right. Maybe I should think about getting a horse of my own."

"How about I take you out for a drink? We can look up horses for sale online. Would you like to do that?" David said as he carefully drew Ellen away from him so he could look at her.

"Yes please, I'd like that," Ellen replied. "Thank you, David."

Ellen began to feel the fizzing sensation within her again as David slowly moved his hand towards her face and gently tucked the lock of hair that regularly slipped out of her plait behind her ear. And then, he leaned forward and kissed her.

Clare

Clare was waiting at the airport arrivals gate. Five minutes ago, the crackly voice on the loudspeaker system announced that Joe's flight had landed safely. And any minute now, Joe, Riley and Molly would walk through the sliding doors. Clare could barely contain her excitement. She was straining to see through the crowd as the many other expectant friends and family members gathered round her; the first passengers were now slowly beginning to trickle out through the doors.

And then she saw them. "Joe, Riley, Molly! I'm over here!" Clare called out, waving madly at them. Little Molly slipped away from Joe and Riley, weaving herself through the swarm of people, and then launched herself at Clare. Scooping her up, Clare buried her face in the little girl's hair and held her close.

"I've missed you so much," Clare said.

"Not as much as I've missed you," replied Molly.

Riley was next, walking towards her with outstretched arms, inviting her in for a hug.

"It's so good to be home," Riley said, squeezing her tightly. "How's Sundance?"

Clare laughed. She had known for certain that Sundance would be the first thing on Riley's mind as soon as she set foot in England. "He's waiting for you at home."

And then Joe, her six-foot two baby boy, bent over and gathered her up in a bear hug, lifting her feet up off the ground.

"Welcome home Joe," Clare said, overjoyed at holding him in her arms for that brief moment. She felt the tension drift away from her, the tension she had unwittingly been carrying for six months, now that her boy was home, safe and sound.

"Hello Mum," Joe replied, placing her back down on the ground. "Let's go home."

The long car journey home was a stark contrast to her solitary journey six months ago. Her battered old Land Rover was filled with excited chatter as they all talked, ten to the dozen, about what they had been up to over the past six months.

"Here we are," Clare announced, finally turning into Hollybrook driveway.

"Home sweet home," said Joe.

"Are those balloons for me? Are we having a party?" Molly asked, spotting the multi-coloured balloons, welcome home banner and their friends gathered on the yard.

"Indeed, we are!" grinned Clare. "Everyone has missed you so much, they wanted to see you as soon as you arrived home!"

Molly was halfway out of the car by the time Clare pulled up and turned off the ignition. She went racing over to see her friends, John, Joseph and Noah.

"Hello everyone," Riley said, smiling and waving to all of her friends. "I'll be with you as soon as I've seen Sundance." She strode off towards his paddock.

The hubbub of the greetings quietened as everyone watched Sundance reunite with Riley.

"Sundance, I'm home," she called.

At the sound of her voice, he instantly cantered elegantly across his paddock to greet her. She rested her head against his, and through the silent air, Sundance nickered, his deep gentle nicker, the one he used only for Riley, the other half of his soul.

Clare noticed, whilst everyone was oooooohing and ahhhhing at Riley and Sundance, that Ellen silently shed one single glistening tear. Clare knew how hard it was for her to return Sundance, and she was pleasantly surprised, and very pleased to see David place his arm around Ellen in a supportive, affectionate gesture, and whisper something in her ear. Clare smiled to herself, as Ellen looked up at David, and rested her head on his shoulder. There was more to David than met the eye, and she liked him. He fitted in well at her yard, and Captain was a dream to have on livery. *David and Ellen make a lovely couple,* she thought. *I'll be getting the gossip out of Ellen later!*

"Joe, this is Matthew," Clare said, proudly introducing her son to Matthew.

Shaking hands, Joe said, "I've heard all about you."

"I've heard all about you, too," replied Matthew, laughing in response.

The party was in full swing, with tasty nibbles being handed out by all the children, music playing softly in the background and animated chatter emanating from everyone.

And then Clare heard Riley's voice ring out across the yard.

"What's that? Oh my gosh, are you and Luke....?"

Grinning like a Cheshire cat, Suzie held out her hand to show off the object that had sparked Riley's question; a beautiful, sparkling diamond ring. "Yes, Luke and I are getting married!"

"A toast to Suzie and Luke," Joe called out, and quickly set about refilling everyone's glasses.

"Oh no, not for me," replied Jem, holding her hand up to prevent the sparkling white wine being poured into her glass of orange juice.

"Jem, are you ill?" Suzie teased. "When have you ever said no to a drink?"

Then very slowly, Suzie looked Jem up and down and Clare could see the penny drop, noticing Jem's slightly expanded waistline for the first time.

"Oh my word you're pregnant!" Suzie squeaked.

"I didn't want to steal Joe and Riley's thunder for their welcome home party, or yours for your engagement," Jem blurted out. "But you're right. I haven't eaten all the cakes. I'm going to have a baby!"

"That's the most wonderful news ever," Suzie replied, enveloping her friend into a hug. "Congratulations!"

"Double celebration!" Joe called out.

"Here, here," everyone called out in reply, eagerly congratulating both of the happy couples.

Clare stood back, to take in this special moment, quietly enjoying the happiness engulfing her and her friends. Everyone had welcomed Matthew warmly into their little friendship group, Ellen and David had become close friends, Suzie and Luke were engaged, and Jem was pregnant! And her Joe was home. Joe, Riley and Molly, all safe and sound, back at home. Clare could not think of a time when she had felt happier, than at that very moment, surrounded by her wonderful family and friends.

Printed in Great Britain
by Amazon